SeaBEAN

SARAH HOLDING

SeaBEAN
© Sarah Holding 2013

Published by
Medina Publishing Ltd
Hope Cottage
Mark's Corner
Newport
Isle of Wight PO30 5UH
www.medinapublishing.com

ISBN: 978-1-909339-12-5

Printed and bound by
TJ International Ltd
www.tjinternational.ltd.uk

printed on environmentally-friendly Munken woodfree FSC certified paper

Thermochromic cover by
LCR Hallcrest Ltd
www.lcrhallcrest.com

Illustrations by
Nina Holding, Louis Holding, Jack Cross, Miles Schneegass

CIP Data: A catalogue record for this book is available from the British Library.

SeaBEAN

Book 1 of the
SeaBEAN Trilogy

SARAH HOLDING

Medina Publishing

Contents

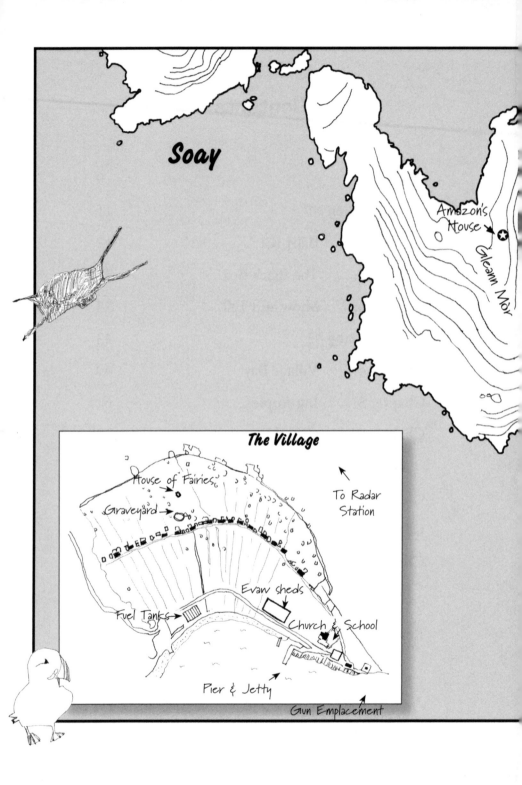

Soay

Amazon's House

Gleann Mòr

The Village

House of Fairies

Graveyard

To Radar Station

Evaw sheds

Fuel Tanks

Church & School

Pier & Jetty

Gun Emplacement

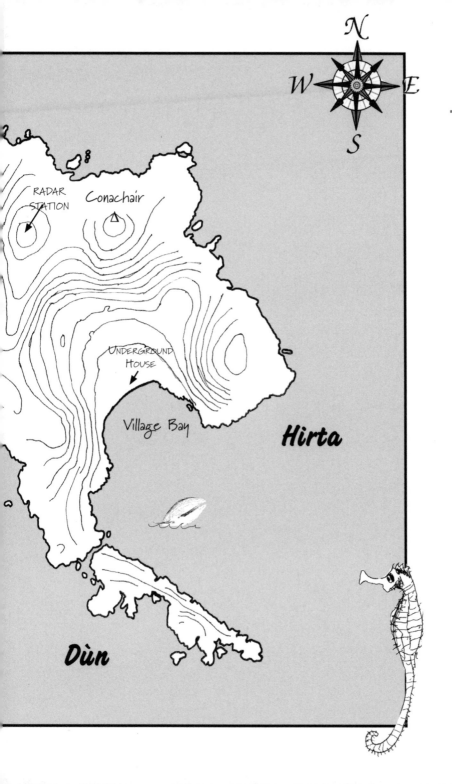

Map of St Kilda

N
W E
S

RADAR
STATION

Conachair

UNDERGROUND
HOUSE

Village Bay

Hirta

Dùn

No one noticed it at first; a strange black object bobbing in the steely grey water, drifting up the Mersey somewhere before daybreak. It was not until it appeared alongside a cruise ship returning from the Caribbean that it attracted any attention.

As the ship docked in Liverpool that dull November morning, the captain reported sighting an 'unexpected navigation buoy' that was not marked on his nautical charts and somehow seemed to be affecting his ship's navigation systems. The Port Authority sent an officer down to investigate, and by lunchtime a curious black cube measuring three metres on all sides was hoisted from the water and deposited on the dockside. It appeared to be not the slightest bit wet and had no identifying marks or features, except that when it was touched by human hands it temporarily changed colour from a dense black to an electric blue.

Tests showed that it failed to transmit a signal either via radar or GPS. The bomb disposal team was called in to carry out a thorough check. The cube-like object was reported as being of unknown origin, constructed of unknown but strangely magnetic materials, probably a foreign buoy that had drifted free from its original mooring. It was scheduled for removal to a landfill site.

Just before midnight, the dockside CCTV cameras picked up some unusual activity. A door opened on one side of the black cube, and a man with white hair stepped out, carrying a battered leather briefcase. The Port Authority failed to locate him with their thermal camera, but when security alerted Merseyside police on suspicion that a man with no staff pass or security clearance had just left the passenger terminal, they took him in for questioning.

Approximately two hours later, the man was released, and no charges were made. He walked out of the police station and, stopping in front of the first postbox he encountered, took a crisp white envelope from his briefcase, posted it, and walked on.

Alice's Blog #1

1st January 2018

My name is Alice. I am ten years old and I live on a really small island called St Kilda, surrounded by weather, waves, and the rest of the world. My new year's resolution is to write a blog about everything that happens here, so people all over the world will be able to read about our life on St Kilda.

Until we came to live here five years ago, no one had lived on our island for eighty-three years. Well, there were some army people stationed here, but that doesn't really count. They were only here to look after the missile detector station on the top of the mountain. It must have been awful in the olden days because it takes hours to come across from the mainland by sea, mainly because the waves are so huge and powerful. But then someone realised they could get energy out of these waves. So now, my Dad, Charlie's dad and some other engineers are going to put wave machines out in the Atlantic near St Kilda, to make electricity for Scotland.

The first thing they did when we got here was build the Evaw shed down by the harbour (that's wave spelt backwards). Next, they are making and testing the wave machines inside it before they put them out in the actual sea.

So nowadays there are exactly ninety-nine people who live on my island, if you include old Jim and the army people. When my baby brother arrives in a few weeks, he will make it a hundred. One, two, skip and few, ninety-nine, a hundred. My Mum and Dad are thinking of calling him Ceud or Kiot, because it means a hundred in Gaelic. They're not Gaelic, and they don't even speak it, but on St Kilda that's what they all used to speak for centuries. Old Jim's the only one here who speaks Gaelic now.

Every hundred hours – well roughly every four days - the ferry comes from the mainland and unloads stuff onto the harbour. The weather is different every day here, so it's often a bit late or not at all, and Mrs Butterfield our shopkeeper goes mad because she's got customers waiting for toothpaste or toilet rolls. Last week they ran out of ketchup, which was a disaster, but Mum says not as much of a disaster as if they run out of nappies when my brother arrives.

My school is also exactly one hundred steps from my house, if you stretch your legs out properly when you walk and you only go in straight lines and do right angles when you go round corners. I usually count it every day, and for the last few weeks it's always been a hundred. When it's raining, I don't count because:

a) I am running in my wellingtons and

b) there are too many puddles to walk in straight lines.

I can't wait for my brother to arrive, because there just aren't enough children on my island. There are only six of us in my class, and my teacher, Mrs Robertson, who is also my Mum, says when we get up to ten she will see about getting us a class pet. Hannah, Edie and I want to get a dog, but the boys, Sam Fitzpatrick (he's the tall one), Sam Jackson (he's the adventurous one), and Charlie Cheung, who is nearly twelve, keep saying they want a fish tank. I think keeping fish in a tank is cruel. Anyway if you want to see fish you just need to go down to the harbour and ask one of the fishermen and they'll open up their polystyrene boxes and show you what they've caught.

7th January 2018

Yesterday we put all our Christmas decorations away. I don't like it much because the house is all bare now. Dad says next year we'll get a real tree with roots from the mainland so that after Christmas we can plant it in the garden and watch it grow. There aren't any trees on our island, so it will be nice to see it blowing in the wind and making a little shadow in our back yard. Mum and Dad say that in the old days the people who lived here didn't even have a word for tree because they'd never ever seen one.

Hogmanay was a lot of fun. That's what we call New Year's Eve in Scotland. There was a big announcement at the party: the people who own our island are giving us the chance to buy it, but they've said we've only got until 1st May to get enough money together – one million pounds – otherwise they're going to let it be sold to this Russian company that wants to set up an oil rig here and drill for oil. Dad says he's not going to let that happen – they're so close to making the wave energy project work, and an oilrig would totally spoil St Kilda.

We have already saved four hundred thousand pounds from all the fund-raising we've done, and then just before Christmas Mr McLintock (the sort of mayor of our island) got a big cheque in the post for five hundred thousand pounds. He doesn't know who it came from, which is a shame because you should really write a nice thank-you letter when someone is as generous as that. Anyway, just to say, if anyone out there has a spare hundred thousand pounds, please let us know, because that's how much we still need, and then we can make our island safe and sound forever!

8th January 2018

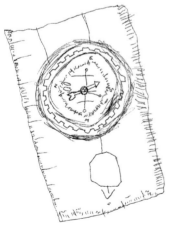

It was our first day back at school today. Mum – I mean Mrs Roberts - let us bring in something we got for Christmas for show and tell. I was going to bring the thing I got in the toe of my stocking. At first I thought it was a walnut or an orange, but it's a sort of smooth brown stone that looks like a miniature hot cross bun. Mum and Dad both asked to have a proper look at it on Christmas Day morning, and they looked really puzzled and said they had no idea where it had come from. That makes it even more special. I have put it in the box beside my bed where I keep my favourite things.

Instead I took in my new watch that's a glow-in-the-dark stopwatch as well as a telling-the-time watch. Edie brought in her new compass, and her little sister Hannah, who's very artistic, brought in some drawings she'd done in her new sketchbook. Sam J got a toy fire engine. It's as red as his hair and is actually an American one because it has a stars-and-stripes flag on the side and says 'Fire Department New York' in big letters, but he insists it's a Scottish one. I suppose he wouldn't know because he's never seen a real fire engine. If there is a fire on our island, Mr McLintock gets in his truck with the hosepipe on the back. Last year, Davie Killigan had a fire in his woodshed, but he'd put it out himself before Mr McLintock got there.

Charlie is still in Hong Kong at his grandpa's while his Dad does some tests on the wave energy equipment there, so we don't know what he got for Christmas. He said he wanted a mobile phone, but I don't see why he needs one when you only need to stand outside your front door and shout if you want to get a message to anyone else around here. He sent me an email today to say it's still hot in Hong Kong, which is funny because it's been snowing a bit on St Kilda.

Mum made a special announcement at the end of the day. I knew she was going to say it because she was talking to Dad last night about how she'd got a letter from the Department of Education or something. She had a sort of sad-but-glad face when she told us she would only be our teacher for another few weeks. The people in charge of Scottish schools are sending over someone called Dr Foster to be our teacher while she is at home looking after my little brother. Mum said Dr Foster was from New York, just like Sam's fire engine.

Dad says that when my brother is born, Granny and Gramps and my big sister Lorina (Lori for short) will come and visit us by helicopter. Dad said he would pay even though it's really expensive, so that they could get here quickly without having to be seasick on the boat for hours and hours. He said as his parents are now both well past seventy it's only right. But it's not fair that Lori gets to go in the helicopter too because she is nowhere near seventy. Lori is going to be fifteen this month. She's at boarding school in Glasgow on the mainland, and so Granny and Gramps are going to meet Lori there and get in a helicopter and fly here.

My brother is due to arrive in between my birthday and Lori's birthday. Lucky Lori was born on 01/02/03 – that's onetwothree. Un Deux Trois, Lori likes to say in a funny accent. I was born on 20/01/07, which is a lot less interesting. Apart from the fact that, if you look on the Internet, it's the day that Barack Obama became president of America in 2009, and it's also the day that someone discovered Adelie Island in Antarctica in 1840. But that's nearly two hundred years ago. Even Granny and Gramps can't remember that.

Anyway, that's the end of my first blog. This is definitely the most I have ever written. Ever.

It was a cold, wet Tuesday afternoon. Alice trailed home from school up the grassy road, dragging her bag along behind her. She felt too tired to count her steps or even care that the bag was getting muddy. On the far side of Village Bay storm clouds gathered, and there was an ominous kind of mood, like something strange was going to happen. All along the top of the cliffs beyond the village she could see flocks of fulmars and other seabirds circling round and round, squawking and diving, unable to settle. In the olden days people had dangled barefoot on ropes off the cliffs to catch them and collect their eggs and even the bird droppings. Alice could hardly believe people would dare to do such a dangerous thing.

Mr McLintock passed in his truck and tooted his horn at Alice. She waved. He leaned out of the window as he drove slowly past up the grassy road.

'You better get home quick lovie, I think your Mum needs you.' He was about to say something else, but then he rolled up the window and stared straight ahead as he moved off down the slope.

Alice hitched her school bag over her shoulder and started walking a little faster. Her Mum always went home early on Tuesdays for an Internet meeting with the teachers from the other Hebridean islands. The vicar, Reverend Sinclair, who was also the pharmacist, taught them history, 'thinking' and Religious Education on Tuesday afternoons. Alice liked doing 'thinking'. The vicar said things like: 'Walruses have moustaches. I have a moustache, therefore I am a walrus.' It made her laugh, even though the vicar was very serious. But she didn't find the history lessons quite so funny.

The vicar told them stories about the past on St Kilda – like the story about how a whole group of islanders decided to leave in 1852 because they were finding life too difficult, so they sailed on a boat called the Priscilla all the way to Australia. He told them there was a place by the sea there, in the city of Melbourne that was also called St Kilda, in memory of the few passengers from the island who survived the terrible journey.

Today the vicar had told them another awful story. The children listened with wide eyes:

'You know, children, for two hundred years most of the babies born on St Kilda died in the first week after they were born, but no one knew why. They think it was because they used to put oil on the babies from fulmars' feathers to keep them healthy, only the oil had got infected and it made them very sick and they died.'

The vicar said that lots of these babies were buried in the village graveyard. After he'd told them the sad story, the children all looked very upset. Alice felt sorry for the vicar, because he couldn't think logically how to cheer them up. But most of all she felt sorry for all the lost babies.

'So children,' the vicar concluded, and he sounded more like the pharmacist talking now, 'The good thing is, that was all a very long time ago, and we have lots of brilliant medicines now to fight all these diseases that babies used to get. Medicines that I have in the pharmacy right here on the island. In the last five years, apart from when young Samuel Jackson here broke his arm, no-one has had to leave the island by air ambulance to go to hospital, which is quite something.'

He looked around. Sam J and Sam F were poking each other with coloured pencils, and Edie was plaiting Hannah's hair. Alice looked at the clock. The vicar followed her gaze, and clapping his hands together said, 'Right then, off you go.'

Alice reached the back door of her house and shoved it open with her shoulder. She dropped her bag by the door and hung up her coat. Her dad was in his slippers pacing round the kitchen on the phone.

'Yes, well, I'd come right away if I were you. No she's fine, thanks. Don't tell Lorina yet.'

'Don't tell Lori what, Dad?' Alice asked.

'Ah, poppet, you're home. Good. Put the kettle on, will you?' Her Dad looked flustered. 'Right, got to go now Gramps. I'll call you later.'

Alice moved slowly around the kitchen finding mugs and swilling out the teapot. Her dad wasn't usually home at this time. She had the feeling that maybe her parents had been arguing, and she hated it when they did. Her mum always said, 'It's being on the island, the long winters, and the never-ending wind, and the being cooped up, it's not natural. Sometimes you just have to let off steam. I still love your Daddy, of course,' she would add, and smile weakly.

'Dad, I need a hug. The vicar told us this horrible story today, and it's made me feel funny…' Alice stopped. Her dad bundled his arms around her and they stood still for a moment in the middle of the kitchen.

'Alice, Mum thinks the baby is coming.'

Silence.

'But it's too early yet, she said so.'

'I know, but you can't choose these things. A baby just comes when it comes.'

'Where is Mum?'

'In bed.'

'Can I go and see her?'

Alice's dad nodded and she went into her parents' room. Her mother was sitting up in bed, still wearing the clothes she'd worn at school.

'Hi Mum. Are you OK?'

'Yes, sweetie. Don't look so worried, it's going to be fine. Jim McLintock has just gone to organise the helicopter for Granny and Gramps and Lori to fly over tomorrow, and Edie's mum is going to come round a bit later to see how I'm getting on. She's delivered lots of babies. Come over here love, you look tired.'

Alice sat beside her mum on the pillows.

'Mum, you've got to promise me something.'

'What's that, love?'

'Wait here.'

Alice ran off to her room and came back with something.

'Close your eyes and hold out your hands.'

Alice placed something in her mother's palm and then folded her fingers around it.

'Right, you've got to absolutely promise me that when my brother is born you won't put fulmar oil on him. Promise?'

Alice's mother opened her eyes wide and looked at her daughter.

'I promise. No fulmar oil. What's all this about?'

'It's not a joke Mum, I'm deadly serious.'

'OK. And what's this? Ah.' Her mother opened her hands and saw a small smooth brown object, shaped like a miniature hot cross bun.

'It's that special stone I got in my stocking at Christmas, remember? It's to bring you good luck. With having the baby and everything.' Alice's mum smiled.

'Thank you Alice, that's very special. You know, I think I know what this is. It's not actually a stone; it's a seabean. I think this kind is called a Mary's Bean.

You find them sometimes washed up on beaches here. Some people look for years hoping to find one.'

That night Alice went to stay over at Edie Burney's house, while Edie's mum, who was a nurse, went to take care of Alice's mum. Normally the two girls chatted non-stop, but both girls were very quiet while they ate tea with Edie's little sister Hannah and Edie's dad. They watched a DVD about tropical rainforests, and then all got in their pyjamas and went to bed.

In the darkness Alice whispered, 'I hope my mum's going to be all right'.

After a while Edie said, 'Just think, by the morning, you'll have a baby brother, you lucky thing'. But by then Alice was already snoring.

The last few hours had been a complete blur: she remembered being woken at eight, and eating half a bowl of corn flakes at Edie's house before running back in her dressing gown and flowery wellies up the grassy slope to her own house. Alice's dad picked her up and swung her round the kitchen so fast he nearly dropped her, and then he laughed, put her down and said, 'Would you like to meet your brother now?'

Alice nodded eagerly. Her dad held the camera above their heads, filming as they walked into the bedroom. Alice's mum was in bed, just like the night before, only now she was wearing Dad's old blue dressing gown, and in her arms was a tight little bundle.

'Alice, come and meet Kit.'

Her brother was all wrinkly and scrunched up, and Alice thought he looked like a caterpillar poking out of its chrysalis. Or should that be a moth? Maybe a bat. He had a soft furry head and little squirrel hands. She hadn't realised he was going to be so small, and was too scared to hold him at first, so she said, 'I want to wait until Lori gets here. She should hold him first, because she's the oldest.'

And now, in a daze, Alice was watching the patterns in the long grass caused by the helicopter's rotating blades. Mr McLintock stood on the shoreline and waved to the helicopter pilot who was trying to land. Alice's dad squeezed her hand as the door opened, and they could see Alice's grandparents inside. Alice jumped up and down and waved in excitement.

Lori ran towards them, bending over to keep out of the way of the helicopter's blades. Granny and Gramps followed, dragging their suitcases across the grass to where Alice and her dad were standing. They all shouted hello to each other but no one could hear anything because it was so noisy. The pilot collected some crates from Mr McLintock and loaded them into the helicopter and then lurched it away.

Back at the house, they had all taken turns to hold the baby, first Lori, then Alice, then Granny and Gramps. Alice couldn't believe how light Kit was, just like the time when she held a baby fulmar chick that had injured its wing. (She was trying her best to put the fulmar oil story out of her mind, but it kept coming back to her.)

Then they all went back into the kitchen to leave Mum in peace to feed Kit. Alice stood next to her sister. They didn't look very alike: Alice had dark hair, pale skin and green eyes, and Lori was much taller with blonde hair, a freckly face and brown eyes. Alice was sure she had got taller even since Christmas, because now she reached up to Lori's shoulder. But she didn't dare say so, in case Lori bit her head off. Well not literally, but Lori often got mad with her. Lori was wearing silver eye make up and pink jeans. She told the story again and again about how she'd tried all night to ring Dad's mobile but the connections were down.

The neighbours came round one by one, the Butterfields, the Burneys, the McLintocks, the Jacksons, the Fitzpatricks, the Killigans, Mrs Cheung and Reverend Sinclair. Granny showed them all the clothes she'd been knitting for her grandson and Dad made them all mugs of tea and handed out leftover Christmas cake. So, thought Alice, this is the day we've all been waiting for in the Robertson family. Wednesday 17th January 2018. She looked on the calendar on the back of the kitchen door. In the square for the 17th was a tiny black circle.

'Daddy, what does that circle mean in the corner of today's square on the calendar?' Alice's father went to have a closer look.

'Ah, that's interesting, it means your brother arrived at new moon, sensible lad.' He thrust his mug of tea in the air like he was about to say cheers and clink glasses with someone, and tea slopped over the side of his mug onto the floor. He didn't even notice, because he was too busy proclaiming a toast.

'To a new baby, a new moon, and a new beginning.' Everyone cheered. Now Alice knew what her mum meant about the cooped up feeling. She needed to get some air all of a sudden.

'I'm going out to see if I can see the new moon,' she said, pulling her coat on.

Outside it was going dark already. The air was very still, and the frost was just starting to turn the grass stiff and sparkly. Alice made her way up past the row of houses to the graveyard and climbed over the stone wall. She sat down on one of the gravestones and looked up. There was no sign of the new moon in the sky, but there were a few stars visible. Alice imagined that each star was the soul of one of the dead babies.

'Poor things,' she whispered, shivering slightly.

After a while she saw colours start to shimmer in the sky, first green, then red and pink, folding and billowing like huge curtains drawn across the sky. It was something Alice had only seen a few times, but she knew for certain what it was.

'The northern lights! It's the northern lights to welcome Kit!' she shouted into the darkness, and ran back to the house to tell her family.

Chapter 2: The Black Box

On the day of her birthday, Alice overslept and her dad had to wake her. She felt a bit cross that she hadn't woken up by herself – usually if something exciting was happening, she would wake before it was even light, even on a Saturday, like today, and rush into her parents' bedroom. Her mum and dad would groan a little, especially if Alice had cold feet, but they would make room for her in the middle so Alice could snuggle down and chatter to them until one of them got up to make the porridge. But today it didn't even feel like an exciting day, let alone her birthday. And she couldn't snuggle into their bed any more really, because by morning the baby was asleep in between her parents.

Alice's dad sat on her bed and handed her a small stack of birthday cards to open – including one from Charlie Cheung sent all the way from Hong Kong. Her dad cleared his throat apologetically.

'Alice, we've got a confession to make: Mum and I haven't got your present yet. I'm sorry love.'

'Uh-huh,' Alice said, trying to keep the disappointment out of her voice until her dad went out of her room. She sighed and then slowly got dressed in her favourite jeans and stripy long-sleeved fleece. Then she opened her birthday cards and took them to show her mum, who was feeding Kit in bed.

'Happy birthday, sweetie,' she said. 'Sorry about your present. Can you wait?' She smiled but looked a bit tired.

'That's OK Mum, don't worry.' Alice perched on the edge of the bed beside her mother and stroked the reddish hair on her brother's soft little head for a minute.

'I'm really hungry now. I'm going to have breakfast with Dad.'

The Robertson's kitchen had an old-fashioned range instead of a cooker and was always lovely and warm. Alice sat at the table where she could see sun shining on the wild sheep in the field in front of their cottage.

'How about some pancakes, birthday girl?' her father asked brightly.

'Yes please! With maple syrup?'

'Don't see why not.' Alice's dad whisked up the eggs, milk and flour. 'Well, poppet, what would you like to do? Shall we go for a walk? The ferry is due in today, you know, with a load of stuff on for my wave energy project, so I'll be down there later. And Mum says Edie is coming over for your birthday tea this afternoon – is that right?

'Mmm.' Alice mumbled. She was in one of those daydreams where you are staring but not looking, and everything is fuzzy.

'I think I want to go for a walk by myself,' she announced after a while. She had a plan to go and see Jim, the old man who lived in the underground house at the end of the village. Everyone said they thought he'd been living there before anyone came back to St Kilda, but it was probably just a story. They also said that Jim was mad as a hatter, but Alice thought he was kind and wise, even though she couldn't understand him because he only spoke Gaelic.

With the last pancake wrapped in a napkin, Alice pulled on her flowery wellingtons and her winter coat and trudged outside. The air was very fresh and the wind was not as noisy as usual. First she walked from her house up the slope past the seven other single-storey houses that had been rebuilt, and then past the seventeen houses that were still ruins. She walked in and out of the empty rooms with no roofs any more and tried to imagine who used to live there. The old crofters' cottages felt lonely and lost. She watched as a little St Kilda wren appeared and started to hop from one stone wall to another, and followed the bird up the hill as far as the old Earth House. She'd heard some people call this the House of the Fairies. There was a thick stone on top of an entrance like a big rabbit hole with some smaller stones surrounding it. Old Jim lived inside.

'Jim,' she called, stepping through the entrance into the earthy interior. 'Are you there? It's me, Alice.'

She could hear Jim shuffling towards her in his worn-out shoes. His beard came down to his waist because he never shaved, and his clothes wrapped round his body like ragged black bandages. She held out the napkin.

'I've brought you a pancake. It's my birthday today. I'm eleven now.'

Jim took the napkin and started eating hungrily. He nodded at her when he'd finished and brushed the sugar from his beard. Then he shuffled off and came back with a tatty red notebook and a pencil. He flicked through the notebook full of what looked like complicated maths and strange diagrams until he found an empty page. There he scrawled a long number – 500,000 – and then pointed at himself with a dirty thumb and nodded vigorously.

Alice giggled and said, 'Oh Jim, you're not that old.'

She said goodbye and went back outside. In the distance she could see the ferry was coming into Village Bay. She checked her watch: ten thirty-two. She tried to work out how long it would take her to run down to the harbour: she wanted to time it just right so she would arrive at the same time as the ferry. Marks, get set, go, Alice whispered, as she pressed the button on her stopwatch and then sped down the hill, jumping over the tussocks of grass. As she whizzed back past the houses, people called out 'Happy Birthday Alice!

In a hurry love?' But Alice just carried on running, keeping her eye on how far the ferry had got as her legs jumbled on.

The St Kilda ferry was a smelly old thing that people on the island are always saying might not get through another winter, but then it turned up again and they were all relieved, because although it was unreliable it was full of all the things they needed, and they looked forward to it arriving. Most families on the island had their own chicken coops, and when they first arrived they brought six cows with them. The cows were kept in a stone enclosure to stop them trampling over all the vegetables, which they also grew in little stone enclosures, to keep the wind off. So apart from milk and eggs, everything else had to come on the ferry.

When Alice got down to the harbour they were already unloading. Ten thirty-eight. It had taken six minutes. She felt disappointed because she had run really fast and now had a stitch. There were the usual shouts from the ferrymen as containers full of things were dragged off the boat along the metal gangway, while the dog that always came with them tried to round everything up. There were no cars on the island, apart from Mr McLintock's truck, so things had to be wheeled off on carts and trolleys. But today there was a new noise to be heard above the constant chugging of the ferry's engine. Alice could hear it grinding and beeping before she could see it: a forklift truck.

Alice's dad was down by the ferry beckoning to the driver of the forklift truck. It was lifting big wooden crates containing the hydraulic wave energy parts, and some other long orange components that her Dad called floats. Alice stood and watched as they brought them up the harbour road and unloaded them outside the Evaw shed. It took five trips to get all the pieces of machinery brought up, and when the crates were all inside, Alice's father rolled the huge doors shut.

Someone shouted, 'There's one more thing, Mr Robertson!'

'No, that's everything.' He pulled a sheet of paper out of his jeans back pocket and checked down a list. But as he was checking it, Alice could see the men lifting another large item with the forklift from right at the back of the ferry's hull. It came out backwards, slowly emerging into the sunshine. The forklift deposited a large and rather peculiar black box on the beach.

'What the dickens is that?' asked her dad.

'Is it OK to leave it here, Mr Robertson?' shouted the forklift truck man, 'only we've had a rough weather warning and we need to get going now.'

'Sure. Leave it there,' Alice's dad called back, scratching his head. 'I'll ask around in the pub this evening – we'll find out whose it is and get it moved.' He shrugged his shoulders, gave Alice's ponytail a playful tug, and then handed her a two-pound coin before he set off back to his office.

'Get yourself a cream cake or something from the shop. See you at teatime Alice!' he called over his shoulder.

Alice stood staring at the box for a moment or two with a puzzled look on her face. In the shop, Mrs Butterfield also stopped unpacking her new stock for a moment and squinted at the black box standing on the beach.

'Whatever is that thing Alice? Does your Dad know anything about it love? Never seen anything like that before. Hope it's not some new piece of military equipment; I thought we were supposed to be getting rid of all that.'

'I'm not sure. It looks really weird, doesn't it? I'm going to go and have a closer look.' Alice chose a nice chocolate éclair and Mrs Butterfield put it in a paper bag for her.

'There you go love, keep your money. It's your birthday, isn't it?' Alice smiled and nodded. She put the coin in her pocket and walked back down to the beach, munching the éclair.

It was the kind of black that Alice imagined black holes would be made out of: so dark you get lost in it. She walked round it several times before she noticed the outline of a door on one side, but no handle. Beside the door was another tiny door just at Alice's eye level. She touched it, and it felt like it was covered in velvet. She noticed that her fingers left little blue marks where she'd touched it. She felt all the way round the edges of the little door and suddenly it popped open. Behind was a bright silver panel with lots of numbered buttons, a tiny slot, a screen and a row of round coloured lights, but they were all switched off. It was like one of those machines she'd seen on the mainland where you get money out. When she closed the door again, it clicked shut and sort of breathed out.

Somehow when she stared hard at it, Alice thought that the edges of the box seemed to wobble, like it was about to disappear. She closed her eyes and quickly opened them again, and that time she thought the box was more like a square hole that had been cut out of the picture. Then she noticed that even though the sun was shining, it was as if it shone on everything except the black box, because around its base it had no shadow.

Alice knelt down and touched the sand next to the edge of the box. It was cold and wet. She started to scrape the sand away from the base of the box, like a dog. When she had cleared away a pile about as big as a bucket, she felt the underneath surface of the black box. The dark velvety metal continued. Pretending to be a forklift, Alice extended her arms straight out in front of her, placed both hands under the box and pressed upwards. Some sand fell away from the underside, and then the box lifted ever so slightly off the ground. She was amazed: how could this enormous metal box be as light as a feather? Suddenly frightened, she quickly pulled her hands away in case the box squashed them, but it paused for a moment before easing itself back onto the sand, and she even thought she heard it make a little sighing noise.

Alice stood up and patted the black side of the box.

'You're a strange one,' she whispered softly. She watched her bluish hand mark slowly fade through all the colours of the rainbow back to black. She drew a circle on the side of the box, but by the time she drew eyes and a smiley mouth, the circle was already disappearing. She stretched out her arms and measured along one side, like she had seen her Dad measure the rooms when they came to visit their cottage for the first time. The box was three times as long as her arm span on each side. From above it would be a perfect square, Alice thought. She stood back, and judged it was about three arm spans high, too. A perfect cube.

The pile of sand from the hole she had dug seemed to spoil the perfectly formed cube, so she started to push it all back under the box and smooth it over. As she did so, Alice came across something hard and shiny. It was a thin, flat rectangle of metal the size of a credit card covered in wet grains of sand. Something washed up in the last tide perhaps, or maybe one of the ferrymen dropped it, Alice thought. She took it down to the water's edge to wash it off and see whether it had someone's name written on it. The water was icy cold, and she dipped the card in quickly, trying not to get her hands wet. She wiped it on the sleeve of her coat and then held it up to dry.

Written in raised letters it said 'C-Bean Mk.3'. On the front there was a hologram image of a globe that shimmered in the sunlight, and then the back of the card was coated in the same dark black as the box itself. Alice walked back towards the box.

'C-Bean Mark 3,' she said aloud. 'Is that what you're called? The C-Bean. And is this your key, perhaps?' She approached the side where the tiny door was, and gently pushed it to make it pop open. Sure enough the slot inside was about the right width to receive the shiny card. As she was about to post it in, the hologram globe on the card started spinning and then the coloured lights on the panel flicked on, turning first red, then orange and then, one by one, green. Alice held her breath and slid the card into the slot.

Chapter 3: Show and Tell

'Not everything is what it seems', drawled Dr Adrian Foster, as he cast his eye over the five children seated in front of him. It was Monday morning, his first day as their new teacher. 'And some things can travel a long way from where they come from to tell us something about other times and other places. They are like little clues that pop up now and again when we least expect it. Like a message in a bottle. Like me, for instance.'

He chuckled to himself and nodded like a toy robot, as if to confirm these statements, fixing his gaze of each of the children in turn. He had curly white hair, wore a grey duffel coat with big deep pockets, and trousers that were a bit too short for him. He wore some kind of identity bracelet on his left wrist, and on his feet he wore white sneakers with fluorescent yellow laces the colour of highlighter pens. Attached to a toggle on his coat he'd tied another yellow shoelace that disappeared into one of his pockets.

As Alice absorbed the different aspects of her new teacher's appearance, Dr Foster pulled a long prickly-looking object out of his other coat pocket.

'I forgot to say, kids, it's Show and Tell today. So I thought I'd bring in something myself, to show y'all.'

Dr Foster passed the object around. 'Take a look at this, everyone, and tell me what you think it is.'

Dr Foster was obviously used to a bigger class than this in New York, Alice thought, because the word 'everyone' sounded silly talking to five children sitting on a small rug.

Sam F flinched when it was his turn to hold it, and said suspiciously 'Yuck, I'm not touching that! What is it anyway?'

Sam J sniffed it, then pretended to comb his mop of red curly hair with it. 'Look Sam, it's a brush.'

'No-o-o, it's not a brush,' said Dr Foster, his eyes twinkling at Sam J's rascally nature. Sam passed it back to Edie.

'It's a bit like a hedgehog,' Edie said, holding it in her lap as if it was a small animal, 'Only more lop-sided.'

'Good job, Edith.'

'Don't call me that. I don't like it.' Edie pushed her glasses up her nose and sniffed.

'Sorry – you prefer Edie do you? Anyone else got an idea?' Dr Foster asked, as Edie passed it to Alice. Alice held it gingerly, and ran her finger along the seam that ran down one side. She shook it, and felt something rattle inside.

'Where did you find it?' she asked.

'How d'you know I found it, erm Ali…?'

'Alice. I dunno. It's just not the sort of thing you would buy in a shop. Not in our shop, anyway.'

'Well, you're right there. I did find it. I like finding things, it's my hobby. Especially things washed up on the beach.'

Dr Foster was looking really quite merry and excited now.

'Is it a sea creature?' Alice was beginning to like her new teacher's curious nature.

'Well, that's what people often think. It does look a bit like a sea creature.'

'So can you eat it?' Sam J asked.

'Not exactly, but you could grow things from it. Shall we open it and see what's inside?'

The children nodded, too intrigued now to speak. Dr Foster pulled on the spare yellow shoelace. He kept pulling at it and at the end of the shoelace was a very special penknife. It was black and silver and very fat, like they had tried to squeeze a lot of different tools into it, but they didn't quite fit and kept poking out.

'I need it back now, Alice.'

She handed the prickly thing to her teacher, and Dr Foster slid open a little knife and pressed the tip of the blade against one end of it. He ran the knife along it in a straight line where the seam was. Then he folded the penknife back into its handle and slipped it into his pocket. Everyone was watching him with wide eyes. Their teacher's head seemed to twitch with the effort of using the knife. He pressed quite firmly and the thing snapped open, like the stiff catch on an old-fashioned purse.

Alice was concentrating on the case, but the other children were pushing each other out of the way to see what had fallen out. On the floor in front of where Dr Foster was standing were six little stones the colour of toast. The children reached out to grab one. Dr Foster picked up the last two and gave one to Alice.

'Well, what d'you know, there are exactly six, one for everyone, including Charlie.'

Alice thought this trick would not have worked so well with Dr Foster's old class, because there would have been too many children for 'everyone' to have got one.

'It's like a wee hamburger,' Sam J said, peering at one.

Dr Foster chuckled. 'And that's just what they're called – hamburger beans. They're a kind of seabean and this is their seedpod, it fell from a tree.'

Alice frowned, remembering the seabean she'd given to her mother, and the C-Bean Mark 3 she'd found on the beach just two days before. There was something strange about this whole Show and Tell thing, but she couldn't work out what it was.

'Where does the seedpod come from?' asked Edie, knowing there weren't any trees on St Kilda for it to grow on.

'Well, it didn't come from this island. Or the next island. Or even the mainland. It came from a cloud forest deep in the Amazonian jungle. Bats drink the nectar of the tree flower, pollinate the plant and the seeds form,' Dr Foster paused to let this image sink in. Alice could see a thick mist forming, and more trees disappearing into the distance than she could ever imagine.

'Dr Foster, how do the seabeans get washed up here then?' Alice asked.

'They are carried by a magical sea current.'

'All the way to St Kilda?'

'All the way.'

Dr Foster turned to the wall behind them where a world map was pinned up. He pointed at Scotland with one hand, and at the Amazon basin in South America with the other.

Moving his hand round and round like he was stirring soup, he said 'you see, the current that connects all your lovely remote islands off the coast of Scotland with the coastline of Brazil where the Amazon meets the sea is a nice warm one, called the Gulf Stream. And when things get swept into the sea, the wind blows and the waves roll and they carry things a long long way.'

'Why?' asked Hannah, looking up from a drawing she'd just done of the prickly pod.

'It's just one of the fascinating things about how our planet works, and it's all to do with the tides, the winds, the moon, and the gravitational pull.' Alice thought for some reason that Dr Foster sounded like he was repeating lines that he'd learned.

'I thought the tide just goes in and out, and that when it goes out the sea gets sort of thicker, and then when it comes in, the sea is thinner,' Edie said, staring at the map.

'Well it's always moving about, and bringing treasure when it returns. Beaches are full of hidden treasure. Like this seabean. I bet if we looked carefully, we'd actually find other seabeans on your beach right here.'

As he said it, Dr Foster looked straight at Alice and raised his eyebrows, as if he knew exactly what she was thinking. It made her feel slightly uneasy. She stared back at him but decided not to say anything.

Dr Foster picked up the fragments of the casing and held them gently in the palm of his hand.

'Do you have a nature table, children?'

Edie stood up to show Dr Foster. She was the Nature Table Monitor.

'It's not got much on it at the moment, because it's winter and there aren't any flowers and stuff to collect outside,' she explained to Dr Foster.

'Well, we can start a new collection, then. Edie, can you arrange it while Alice makes up an identification card, please?'

He gave Alice a small white card and a black pen. She pictured the word 'seabean' in her head, and quite liked the way it had two lots of 'ea' in it. When she had finished writing she was disappointed though, and even thought about asking Dr Foster for another piece of card, because the n had ended up too close to the right-hand edge. She propped the card in front of the seedpod on the table and then, after a moment of hesitation, put her hamburger seed next to the pod, because that's where it seemed to belong.

Dr Foster wasted no time on his first day getting to know not just the children but the island as well. Straight after morning break, he said that it was their turn to do a Show and Tell. The children protested and said they had not brought anything to show, so Dr Foster told the children to put on their coats and said they were to take him on a tour of the island.

'But it's too big! It'll take too long,' moaned Sam F.

'Well then, just show me the best bits,' suggested Dr Foster reasonably.

'What about our shop – have you seen that yet?' Edie asked.

'Yes, I went there yesterday to get some shampoo, as it happens.'

Alice was relieved when she heard this, because the one thing she didn't want to have to show Dr Foster was her C-Bean, and he was sure to notice it.

'Do you want to climb our wee mountain – the Conachair?' Sam J wanted to know.

Dr Foster laughed, 'Maybe not today, Sam, but maybe this weekend.'

'How about the First World War gun – have you been to see that?' Sam F asked, getting into the idea.

'Now that sounds like something I gotta see,' agreed Dr Foster. 'Alice, are you coming with us?'

Alice was sitting in the corner of the classroom by the nature table, with a faraway look on her face. Now that the C-Bean had arrived, the island seemed different, like another place. Come to think of it, now that Kit had arrived, home seemed like somewhere else too. And today, school felt strange; Mum wasn't there, and that was both good and bad. There was just a lot of newness to get used to.

As they set off it started raining in a slow steady drizzle. Alice was hoping they would not head for the beach where the C-Bean was. She didn't want Dr Foster to find it. At least, not yet. Thankfully, they headed out of the village away from the beach. Dr Foster had brought a large golf umbrella and the children crowded underneath it as they walked past the first of the cottages and on up the hill to the west. The weather closed in until they could only see about two houses ahead. They showed him the repaired houses with their new turf roofs, and the children pointed out whose was whose. Then they passed the graveyard. Alice hoped no one would want to tell Dr Foster about the babies buried there.

Edie just said as they passed, 'That's where the people who used to live on St Kilda are buried'.

Next they passed the ruined houses and the boys told Dr Foster all about how they had beds that were built into the walls and slept on straw and bits of turf instead of mattresses in the olden days.

Dr Foster listened intently as he trudged on up the hill. 'Heck, you kids know a lot about this island! And what are all these little stone huts?'

'They're called cleitean or cleits. It's where they kept all their food and stuff,' said Sam F.

Alice had fallen behind the others. They were approaching old Jim's underground house. She ran to catch up. As Alice got closer, she could smell Dr Foster's wet duffel coat. It was like an old dog.

'Dr Foster?'

'Yes, Alice?'

'Have you met Old Jim?'

Dr Foster was panting a little as they walked up the hillside. Alice also noticed that his left knee clicked when he walked. He straightened up suddenly, holding the umbrella up high with one hand and putting his other hand against his back to support himself for a moment.

'Erm, no, don't think we've been introduced. Who's Jim?'

'He lives in an underground house just up here. He's my friend,' Alice said.

'Well, maybe I'll meet Jim some other time. I think I've had enough of an introduction to this weather. Shall we head back, kids?'

'Just a moment.'

Alice skipped on ahead and stooped down in front of the entrance to the underground house and called into the darkness, 'Hello? Jim, are you in there?' Alice stood waiting but there was no reply.

The rain had become heavier and more persistent and they began to make their way back down to the village. When they got back to the classroom, Dr Foster went into the back room and came back with a huge roll of paper. He suggested they made a big map of the island for the rest of the day, and that they should all mark onto it the other places they'd not yet managed to show him. Sam F made the first move by drawing on the gun emplacement on the headland, pointing the gun out to sea.

'You know, Dr Foster, the gun has never ever been fired,' Sam said solemnly. He harboured a secret hope that one day, when he was old enough to be one of the army men himself, he might be called upon to fire it.

Edie wrote a list for Dr Foster of all the people on the island, starting with the McLintocks, the Jacksons, the Killigans, the Fitzpatricks, the Butterfields, the Robertson, the Cheungs, and her own family, the Burneys. Next to each person's name she wrote down what they did. It was not a very long list of names, but since everyone had more than one job, it took a long time to write. Then she wrote little numbers next to the names and corresponding numbers on the map showing where they all lived or worked, or both. For Charlie Cheung, she also wrote an email address, because he was still in Hong Kong.

Sam J decided the map should be more three dimensional, and went to get the building blocks out. He put one yellow cube for each cottage, two green ones each for the shop, the church and the school, red ones for the two rows of army huts and, down by the harbour, eight blue blocks to make up the Evaw shed where the wave energy machines were being built. Hannah meanwhile made some very detailed drawings of all the shells you could find along the beach, and all the different kinds of birds that lived on St Kilda. Then she cut them out and put them all around the edges of the giant map.

Alice looked at their efforts. It seemed too bland and ordinary with just the blocks and the list. Even with Hannah's drawings it didn't begin to explain their amazing island. She put some cotton wool on the hillside, to make it seem more like the kind of cloudy wet day Dr Foster had just experienced. Then she made a little enclosure out of salt dough to form the graveyard, and a mound with an entrance to mark on the map where Jim's underground house was.

It was almost finished, and the children were tired. Dr Foster said they could go on their laptops until it was time to go home. Alice checked her email. There was one from Charlie, sent the day before.

Hi Alice. Who's the big sister now then! Let me know what our new teacher is like. Is it snowing or raining? Hong Kong is still full of tourists. Everybody comes here to go shopping, even on Sundays. Got to go. See you in a few weeks! Charlie.

He had attached a picture of himself holding his new mobile phone, standing in a street full of traffic in front of a tall grey building with lots of people walking across a bridge in the background. Alice wondered what the map of Hong Kong Island would look like compared to St Kilda. She tried to imagine the crowds of shoppers, the noise of cars and buses, the feel of the pavements.

As they were all packing up, Alice found a small black cube of Lego on the floor. She picked it up: this was what was missing from the map. In front of the shop, beside the sea wall, she placed the black cube right where the C-Bean had been left.

Alice's Blog #2

22nd January 2018

So there have been three arrivals actually, not just two. Baby Kit isn't even supposed to be here yet. But he is: by my watch, he's already more than 100 hours old. And, of course, I'm now eleven years and two days old.

The second new arrival is Dr Foster. His knee clicks when he walks and he looks a bit like a sheep. He even sounds a bit like a sheep when he laughs.

But something else has arrived too. There's a very strange cube thing on the beach called a C-Bean. It arrived on my birthday, and so I really thought it was somehow meant to be my birthday present. I mean I kind of decided it was mine: it didn't seem to belong to anyone, and nobody knew what it was.

I bet you're wondering what happened when I went inside it! I wasn't going to write about this, but as it's part of what's happening in my life here, I suppose it should be in my blog.

Imagine stepping inside a whale. Except on the inside there are walls and a floor and a ceiling that keep changing all the time. It was as if it was recording everything about me: how big I was, how I moved, how hot I was, what my voice sounded like and what mood I was in. I bet you're thinking: how did she know it was doing all that? Well, first of all the walls showed my outline, like I was casting a shadow on them, except there was no light shining on me to make the shadow. Then it put the shadow into colours, and I noticed my hands and face were coloured blue (where I was still cold from outside), but my body was red. If I walked around, the shadow images moved around as well on all four walls.

When I said 'hello' the C-Bean echoed like I was in an enormous cave. I said it in all kinds of silly voices and the C-Bean kept repeating whatever I said back to me. Then, when it had got all the information about me it needed, it projected a hologram that was exactly the same size and shape as me into the middle of the room and I could walk all the way round her. I tried to touch the hologram but it wasn't made of anything except coloured light projected in the space. Then I said hello again, and the 3D picture of me said hello back. Then she started copying anything I did, but doing the mirror image, so if I moved to the left, she moved to the right.

I stayed inside the C-Bean for ages, and it felt like I'd made a new friend. I realised I'd got quite thirsty. I didn't say it out loud or anything, but a few seconds after I thought about wanting a drink, this little opening appeared in one wall, like the hatch in one of those vending machines. A fresh glass of water stood there waiting for me. I picked it up and drank it. Then, to test it, I began to picture in my head a chocolate biscuit. The opening disappeared for a moment or two and then reopened, and there on the shelf was just the kind of biscuit I had been thinking about. It was delicious.

After that I imagined all sorts of things, like a pen, a camera, an electric toothbrush, a baby's rattle. Every time, whatever I had imagined would appear, in exactly the same colours and shapes that I'd pictured in my head. Next I tried things that were a bit bigger, like a guitar or an umbrella, to see if they would fit in the hatch. When the opening reappeared it was just longer or larger. Then I tried to think of something more particular, like our St Kildan postage stamps, or my own teddy, but it managed fine. Teddy looked a bit too clean, though.

Then I thought: if it can do a stuffed toy animal, can it do a real one? That was clever: the real animals appeared, but they were just holograms and images. I had zebras stampeding all around me. I stood in amongst a herd of elephants spraying each other and washing themselves. I watched hundreds of penguins diving off an iceberg right in front of me into the sea. It was so real – you could smell the fish they were eating and hear all the sounds they were making and the room got colder and colder as I watched the sun set over Antarctica. When the room was completely dark, I suddenly wondered if it had gone dark outside the C-Bean too. I picked up the rattle to give to Kit and opened the door to go out.

The sun had set outside too. I could still feel the rattle in my hand when I stepped out onto the sand, but by then it was already invisible, I could only hear the rattling sound until I got as far as Edie's house. By the time I reached our house, it had completely disappeared.

When I woke up the next morning I remembered I'd left the card key in the slot of the C-Bean. After Dad and I had been to church (Mum stayed at home with Kit, but she did at least get dressed), he went off to a meeting in the pub about buying the island, so I said I'd walk back by myself. I waited until he'd gone inside the pub, then I ran down to the beach. I was really scared the C-Bean might have gone, but as soon as I came round the corner past the shop, I could see its straight black edges against the sky.

I walked slowly up to the C-Bean and suddenly felt shy. The big door was shut. I pressed the little door on the panel next to the door and it opened like before and I could see the card was still inside the slot. I pressed some of the buttons but none of them made the card come back out, and anyway the lights had gone out. I walked round the outside to see if there was any other way of getting in, or if it had changed colour or shape at all on the outside, but it was the same smooth matt black on all four sides with no reflections. I went back round to the door and slumped up against it, feeling very disappointed that I couldn't get back in. I felt the door nudge me, and when I turned round, I saw my body had left a blue mark on the surface where I had been leaning. Then I heard my own voice say hello. I said hello back and the door opened. It remembered me! I was about to go back inside, but then I thought how much fun it would be to show Edie, so I closed the door and ran off to fetch her.

It was a real shame, because Edie had a temperature and her Mum said she had to stay indoors. Also, my mum had come round to see where I was. I felt bad that I hadn't gone straight home, and that Mum had to bring little Kit outside because of me. So I went home and helped Mum make Sunday dinner.

23rd January 2018

Just after lunchtime today there was a lot of noise and when we looked out of the window, Mr McLintock was unloading something from the back of his truck into the school yard. Everyone crowded round the window to see what was going on. Dr Foster went outside to find out, and when Mr McLintock had driven off, he came back inside rubbing his hands together, all excited about something.

He said something like, 'Well, kids, that strange-looking thing outside is our new ultra high-tech classroom.' Then he said, 'We are very lucky indeed. It's a gift from an anonymous donor to help the children of St Kilda. None of the other islands has one.'

I looked through the window and realised with a shock what Mr McLintock had delivered to the yard: my C-Bean! I couldn't quite believe what Dr Foster was saying, and anyway calling it a classroom made it sound very boring. Plus it didn't look nearly as exciting in our schoolyard as it did when it was down on the beach. It also looked a lot smaller.

Dr Foster said the instruction manual was supposed to be arriving by post so until then he had no idea how to use it. I was about to put my hand up and tell him I knew how to open the door, but I stopped myself just in time. I felt a bit confused. Part of me felt it was my C-Bean, my present, my secret. But part of me couldn't wait for the others to see inside and find out about all the amazing things it could do.

24th January 2018

My birthday present from Mum and Dad arrived in the post this morning: it was a big globe that swivels on an axis and has a light inside. It is designed to get brighter and brighter by itself in the morning to wake you up. I've put it beside my bed, so I can look at all the places I want to go one day before I fall asleep. Lori gave me some yummy chocolates and Granny and Gramps gave me a 1000-piece jigsaw with a picture of the other St Kilda in Australia that they'd found on the internet. It has a very nice beach with palm trees, but for a jigsaw it's got a bit too much plain blue sky.

Lori went back with Granny and Gramps on the helicopter on Friday. Part of me wanted to go back with Granny and Gramps and stay with them for a while. They live in Liverpool in a block of flats overlooking the River Mersey. Another part of me wished I was older and that Lori and I were going back to boarding school together in Glasgow, and that I had lots of friends and clothes and make up like Lori. But the biggest part of me wanted to stay here and be with Mum and Dad and Kit. Even though the walls aren't quite thick enough between my bedroom and theirs when Kit cries at night. Also, we are eating a lot of things out of tins, not because Daddy can't cook, but because right now he's either:

a) looking after Mum and the baby or

b) down in the Evaw shed.

He keeps saying 'It's a critical time right now,' but no one is being critical at all. Mum is extra specially kind and lovely at the moment. It's probably because she didn't get out of bed for three whole days.

Anyway, my presents weren't the only things that arrived on the ferry this morning: the C-Bean's instruction manual came in the post too.

On Wednesday morning, Mr Butterfield, who delivered the mail round the island after it arrived off the ferry, brought a package for Dr Foster. It was a bright calm day, and he stood around chatting in the schoolyard for ages. As far as Mr Butterfield was concerned, this was all part of doing a good job as the island postie, and many other messages and pieces of information were entrusted to him on the doorsteps of St Kilda.

Eventually Dr Foster came back into the old classroom with the large brown envelope tucked safely under his arm. Alice's heart skipped a beat when she saw the hologram symbol of the Earth printed on the top left corner of the envelope, the same design as on the key she'd found on the beach. Dr Foster tore open the envelope and pulled out a large black folder full of information about the C-Bean Mark 3.

The children were supposed to be doing some maths exercises, finding number patterns using their hundred squares, which Alice usually loved. But as soon as Dr Foster emptied the envelope they all stopped what they were doing and watched him intently. Alice could feel a noise like waves crashing inside her and she began to feel as if she was breathing underwater. Her secret was about to be revealed.

The night before Alice dreamed about the C-Bean. In the dream, she was back inside it, imagining being in Antarctica again. The C-Bean started to move around like an iceberg in the sea, and she kept slipping from side to side every time it moved. The penguins seemed to be getting further and further away, and then she could see one being tossed high into the air, and suddenly a huge whale came bursting through the wall of the C-Bean, spouting water and lunging towards her. She was gasping for air, and when she reached out to try and save herself, all she kept grasping were babies' rattles, only they weren't like a child's plaything because they were covered in this thick, smelly oil.

When Alice woke, she was breathing heavily as if she had run all the way down the hill to the shop. She opened her eyes and saw the light from her globe and let her eyes adjust while she tried to convince her brain that she was not in the Antarctic, even though her bedroom was so cold she could see her breath. She wondered if she had shouted out loud in the nightmare, because she could hear her parents stirring next door, and Kit starting to whimper. She slid on her slippers and went out into the passageway.

'Mum? Dad? Are you awake?'

'Go back to sleep Alice. It's OK, we're just changing Kit's nappy,' her Dad said in a loud whisper.

'Can I come in your bed? I've had a nightmare.'

'Umm. Well, Mum's a bit tired. Just a minute and I'll come and tuck you in, love.'

Alice stood shivering for a moment, then ran back into her room, jumped into bed and buried her head under her pillow to stifle her tears. In the morning she still had her slippers on.

The C-Bean's instruction manual came in the form of a digital tablet in a smart case, and there was also a small printed booklet containing a 'Quick

Start Guide'. Tucked into a pocket inside was another thin metal cardkey identical to the one Alice had used.

Dr Foster laid it all out on his desk and said, 'Well, kids, where shall we start?'

'How do we get inside?' Eager as ever, Sam J blurted out the question uppermost in all their minds.

The C-Bean stood, dark and silent, in the middle of the cracked concrete yard. Alice noticed yesterday that on one side there was a nasty scrape mark where Mr McLintock's truck had winched the C-Bean down with his tow chain and his hook had caught against it. When she touched the scrape mark, the black surface felt spongier around where it had been damaged, and a silvery crust had formed over the surface. After school was over, Alice got a sponge and some warm water from the classroom sink and tried to clean the wound a little. The warm water turned the black surface a vivid electric blue, like the sky on a cloudless day, but it didn't seem to get wet at all. Instead, when she had finished sponging the surface, it just returned to being the densest black imaginable.

'Why don't you all go out in the yard and have a good look for some kind of slot for this cardkey then, while I have a quick read of the instruction guide, and see if we can work it out.'

The children wasted no time. Sam J grabbed the key from Dr Foster's desk and tussled with Sam F to be first out of the door, with Edie close behind holding her new compass and shouting instructions bossily to the two boys. Hannah was busy drawing flowers.

'Hannah, Alice, come!' called Edie, turning back. But both girls stayed put. As far as Hannah was concerned, unless the new classroom was full of paint, paper, pens and pencils, she would not be interested. Alice just wanted to delay the moment when the C-Bean was no longer hers alone. She stared at her hundred square and started counting. She had made a bet with herself that it was bound to take until she got to a hundred before they found the slot for the key. Or at least, that was how long she was prepared to give the others before she went outside and opened the C-Bean for them … ninety-eight, ninety-nine, a hundred. When her finger was on the last space, Alice looked up from her desk. From where she was sitting she couldn't see any of the children out of the window.

She walked outside, calling 'Are you in yet?'

'Nope. Round here.' They were on the far side of the C-Bean, lying face down on the concrete trying to slide the card key underneath the C-Bean.

'Edie thought she could see a little gap just down here.'

'Hmm,' said Alice, 'shall I have a go?'

They handed her the key and she walked up to the door and said in a loud voice, 'HELLO'. She was not sure what she expected to happen. There was a pause, and then the smaller door eased open and the lights flickered on one by one.

'Wow,' said Edie. 'How did you do that?'

'Look, there's a key already in the slot!' Sam J yelled, jumping up and down and clapping his hands together.

Alice paused. The boys were already hammering on the main door, waiting for it to open. She looked down at the other cardkey in her hand, with its globe spinning away. She slipped it into her cardigan pocket

'Hello,' she breathed so quietly no one but the C-Bean would hear.

Edie was looking down at her compass. 'Look you guys! Look at this!'

Just as the C-Bean's door opened, the north point on the compass started flicking back and forth, and then started spinning furiously.

'Maybe this thing's made out of something magnetic,' suggested Sam F.

'Well?' said Sam J, poking his head inside the door. 'Are we going inside or what?'

'We'd better get Dr Foster first,' said Edie.

Edie was just about to go back inside the school when Dr Foster emerged, followed by Hannah.

'Ah, you've managed to get it to open. Fabulous.'

So, for the second time, Alice stepped inside the C-Bean ...

It was as dark and as cold as when she had left it after her Antarctic adventure, but Alice felt hot with anticipation. Dr Foster was trying to find a light switch.

Alice cleared her throat. 'We need some LIGHT,' she said slowly and clearly.

The room started getting lighter so slowly that at first the children all thought their eyes were just getting used to the gloom, like when your parents turn off the lights at bedtime. But after a minute the ceiling, the floor and all four walls started glowing faintly, just bright enough for the children to see the dumbstruck look on each others' faces as they took in their new surroundings.

The inside of the C-Bean was absolutely empty. There was nothing on the floor, or the walls, no shelves, no cupboards, no books, no art trolley, no computers and no furniture. Dr Foster began to look a bit impatient.

'Where's all the stuff?' asked Sam J, reading his teacher's mind.

'Well, on page five of the manual it talks about a Central Resource Table, but I don't see any table!'

'CENTRAL RESOURCE TABLE,' repeated Alice. The two Sams, who were standing in the middle of the C-Bean, began to rise up from the floor on a platform about the size of a double bed.

'Cool!' they chimed. They both laughed and began to tap a slow rhythmic beat on the top of the table between them, and parts of a grid of coloured lights appeared where they'd touched the surface.

'It's a hundred square!' exclaimed Alice. The boys slid off the table and the children found they could fill in the gaps by touching the table here and there, and then watched as different mathematical sequences rippled in rainbows across the square. Once it had completed all the times tables, the table went white.

Under the table was a kind of pit, so the children could sit around it and tuck their legs underneath. Dr Foster sat down too and took off his glasses. Where they rested on the table Alice noticed a tiny coloured outline forming.

'Edie, can you put your compass on the table for a minute?' she asked. Edie took the compass from around her neck and placed it in front of her. The north point was still twitching. A two-dimensional copy of the compass started appearing in the surface of the table. Even Dr Foster was wide-eyed now.

'It's like it can record things,' said Sam F, 'but I bet it doesn't know what they're for.'

'What is a COMPASS for?' Alice asked, and Sam was about to answer the question, thinking it was directed at him, when the table displayed a whole series of moving diagrams of the Earth involving the North and South Poles, with arrows looping from one pole to another. But there were no sounds or words to explain anything.

Dr Foster, his eyes fixed to the table, said 'Ah, it's trying to tell us about magnetic north and how the Earth is like a giant magnet. Your compass is magnetised too, Edie, so that it will always know where north is, and you can use it to work out what direction you are facing.'

Alice thought that Edie's compass was not at all sure where north was at the moment.

Dr Foster continued, a little breathlessly, 'I wonder if there's meant to be sound too? I didn't notice a section about that in the manual. Come to think of it, it did mention a new kind of interactive whiteboard, but I don't know which wall it is – they all look the same.'

'Maybe it doesn't matter which wall you write on,' Alice mused silently to herself, 'but you'd need a PEN.'

A moment after Alice had the thought, a hatch appeared in the wall nearest to Dr Foster to reveal a whiteboard pen. The children watched in disbelief as Dr Foster put his glasses back on and reached out to pick up the whiteboard pen. The hatch then closed up and disappeared.

'Terrific, just what I needed,' Dr Foster laughed, trying to pretend this was nothing out of the ordinary. He stood up in front of the white wall beside him and enquired, 'Does anyone know what latitude and longitude are?'

Edie was first to put her hand up. 'Latitude goes this way,' she said spreading her arms sideways, 'and longitude goes that way,' she moved her arms up and down.

'Good. That's right. Longitude tells you where you are on the earth in terms of east or west, and latitude is a way of saying how far towards the North or South Pole somewhere is. It's a coordinate system. Does anyone want to guess what the coordinates are for St Kilda? What I mean is, how far north, and east or west are we? Anyone?'

No one responded.

'No, I didn't know either, so I looked it up last night at Reverend Sinclair's house. He has some real nice books about St Kilda. I found out that we are 57 degrees 48.5 minutes North, and 8 degrees 34 minutes West. Alice, could you write that up here for me?' Dr Foster tapped the white wall and handed her the pen.

Alice wrote the coordinates slowly and carefully on the smooth white wall. She remembered about the Seabean card she was asked to write for the nature table. This time there was plenty of space and the letters could be as big as she wanted. She even put a full stop after the W, but then the pen stopped working properly. Or was it the wall?

Somehow the pen seemed to sink in, as if the whiteboard was soft, like a pillow. Alice touched the surface and it felt damp. She could see her fingers sinking into the space of the wall, and her hand was somehow misting over. She pushed her arm in further until she could no longer see her hand at all.

'Alice, what on earth are you doing?' Dr Foster tried to pull her back, but by then Alice's head had disappeared. Her whole body became enveloped in a kind of thick cloud that was starting to billow into the C-Bean. The other children could hardly see each other through the fogginess, and they reached out to hold each others' hands. But it was too late to hold Alice's hand – she had somehow vanished.

Alice felt a bit dizzy and wondered if this was how it would feel to be caught in a snowstorm, or to jump out of a helicopter in the middle of a thick white cloud. Tiny beads of water clung to her skin, particularly, she noticed, round her ankles. She took a couple of steps, and realised she was wading in icy cold water. Where was she? Not outer space, she decided, as there was very little water there. The air smelled very fresh, like sea air. There was a kind of crying in the distance. She strained her ears to listen, and the crying got louder until she realised it was a seabird calling. She closed her eyes and listened again. Gone. When she opened them, the mist seemed to be clearing, and she could see the rippling surface of the water stretch away in front of her. Behind her the mist was still a thick blanket.

She looked down at her feet submerged in the water, which was extraordinarily clear and was beginning to lap round her knees. Here and there fish darted in silver shoals just above the seabed. She scuffed the white sandy bottom with the edge of her shoe, and caught sight of something black in the water. She reached down to pick it up. A crisp black rectangle with long tendrils trailing from all four corners came up, dripping wet and shiny.

'Alice, where are you?' a voice called. She had almost forgotten about her classmates. Edie's face appeared in the mist, taut with worry.

'Over here,' Alice called, pushing the rectangular thing into her pocket.

Edie waded across, shivering in her waterlogged shoes and tights. Her hair clung in wet straggles round her face and her glasses were all steamed up.

Village Bay

'What are we doing out in Village Bay, Alice?'

'What?' Alice scanned the clearing horizon, and caught sight of the army huts on the foreshore, then the row of little cottages behind, and beyond that the familiar outline of their mountain, Conachair. She felt cheated suddenly. Why here? If the C-Bean could conjure up such vivid images from as far away as Antarctica, why had it deposited them on St Kilda?

'But I thought ...'

'We'd better go back to the C-Bean. Dr Foster will be worried.'

Alice followed Edie into the densest part of the mist, and within moments stumbled back into the small square space with its central table. Hannah and the two Sams were huddled on top of the table in their bare feet, while Dr Foster was standing with his trousers rolled up in the flooded C-Bean, squeezing out their soaking wet socks and hanging them over on the edge of the table.

'Oh girls, thank the Lord! Where did you go? There's been a flood. I don't know where all this water came from. Now let's get back to the schoolyard and dry out.'

'But ...' Alice wanted the others to see what she and Edie had seen. She turned back to the misty wall, but it had already hardened over.

'No buts now. You look half frozen, dear. Whatever would your mother say if she knew I let you all get soaked on my first week here?'

Alice sighed, and did as she was told: 'SCHOOLYARD!' Her voice was clear, but had a slightly tearful wobble. It sounded to the others like a protest, but to the C-Bean it was a firm command. There was a sudden jolting movement, and the door flapped open. The children all exited from the C-Bean, tiptoed barefoot across the cracked concrete and back into their warm old classroom.

After lunch, while their socks were steaming on the radiator, Dr Foster had them all outside again in their dry PE trainers, bailing the C-Bean out with the mop bucket and some plastic containers they kept the coloured pencils in.

Alice noticed that the C-Bean now had a white salty tidemark running all the way round it about twenty centimetres up from the bottom. She looked down at her legs, then measured them with a ruler: if the water had come up to her knees, that meant it was thirty centimetres deep where she'd been standing. If the tidemark on the C-Bean was less, then it must have been floating.

'My compass!' said Edie suddenly. She ran back inside the C-Bean, and reappeared with it hanging round her neck. 'Thank goodness,' she said, 'the north arrow's pointing north again now. Look.' Alice could tell Edie had been quite unsettled by their little adventure. She put her arm round her.

'Shame we didn't get to take a picture of us two out in the Bay, Edie. You looked so funny standing there in the water. Good job it didn't happen in one of those force nine gales!'

Edie said airily, 'I don't even want to think about it. It was too weird. As far as I am concerned, it didn't really happen.'

'It did happen Edie, I know it did. And it's our secret.' Alice reached into her pocket and pulled out the black object she'd found in the water. 'Here, you can have this as a souvenir.'

Edie took hold of the thing by one of its corners and held it up to inspect it. Dr Foster looked across the yard, leaning on the mop handle.

'What have you got there, you two? May I have a look?'

Edie showed her teacher. 'What is it? Alice just gave it to me.'

'Ah yes, that's a mermaid's purse. Dogfish lay their eggs in it, and when the time is right, the eggs hatch, and the little fish just swim on out.' Dr Foster paused, but Edie didn't say anything. 'Why don't you put it on the nature table, Edie?'

'Can I write a name card for it, like Alice did for the Seabean pod?'

'Sure – there's just time before you all go home. Let's go find the right pen. Not like that pen in the C-Bean. We need one that writes like it's supposed to.'

Alice watched as Edie and Dr Foster went back into the school with

Hannah following after them. Sam J and Sam F were bouncing a tennis ball around the schoolyard to each other.

'Watch out,' said Alice, 'we don't want to damage the C-Bean again.'

Something had happened today, something real, something special. The other adventures she had in the C-Bean on the first day, they were imaginary. But today it had somehow transported them from the schoolyard to somewhere out in the bay and back again. It can't have just been an illusion. What about the wet socks, the flooded floor, and the mermaid's purse? So, if it did happen, how did it happen?

Alice went back into the school. The instruction manual lay open on Dr Foster's desk at the page about the Central Resource Table. She touched the menu at the side of the screen and flicked to the index. She noticed there was a listing for 'Using the Interactive Whiteboard' and, lower down, another one titled 'Activating the Transportation Function'. Her heart did a strange sort of flutter as she read it.

'Dr Foster …' she began.

'Yes, dear?'

'Could I take the manual home this evening and read it?'

'I don't see why not, Alice. Then maybe you could you give us a proper tour of where everything is and how it's actually supposed to work. I guess we must have done something wrong today.'

'OK,' she said, her hands shaking with excitement as she stuffed the digital book into her schoolbag. 'I'll bring it back tomorrow.'

When Alice got home from school, her mum was cooking tea while Kit lay in his basket waving his arms. Alice knelt down to tickle his toes. She watched his little face as he wriggled with pleasure.

'Mum, just think, Kit's a week old today.'

'I was just thinking the same thing, sweetheart. What a week, eh!'

'Yeah.' Alice was looking at Kit's face, but she was somewhere else, her eyes had gone fuzzy, and all she could see was his outline against the red blanket. 'I've had such a strange day at school.'

'What's Dr Foster got you doing, then?'

'You know that cube thing they delivered off the ferry? Well it turns out it's for us. It's a mobile classroom that someone's sent over as an experiment, and Dr Foster let us go inside it for the first time today. Did you know it was coming, Mum? It's called a C-Bean, and it's very strange. It's totally empty so you have to imagine things, and then they sort of happen. I can't explain it really. Anyway, Dr Foster has lent me the instruction manual to read this evening.'

'No, it was never mentioned to me,' her mother replied vaguely.

Alice was thinking about the C-Bean all through her meal, and it wasn't until she'd eaten all her sausages and mash she realised she hadn't put any ketchup on her plate. Kit had fallen asleep in his basket and her parents were busy talking about the Evaw plant, so Alice was able to slip away to her bedroom straight afterwards.

She lay down on her bed. The manual contained a lot of long words, and they were all repeated in Spanish, German and Chinese. In the first section, Alice learned that the C-Bean had been designed in Germany and assembled in Brazil. It was a Mark 3 product, which meant that it was replacing the first and second versions they'd made. Ninety-nine new features had been added. (Why not a hundred, Alice thought, they only needed to think of one more!) She skipped ahead to the section on Activating the Transport Function. First there was a long list of things *not* to do when trying to use this particular function. It said things like, 'DO NOT use a mobile phone or other mobile 5G handheld devices in the C-Bean'; 'DO NOT try to transport C-Bean to more than one place at a time'; and 'DO NOT use the reset function if the C-Bean is in motion'.

There were too many diagrams of how the electronics worked and page after page of explanation. Alice couldn't understand why anyone would want to make a set of instructions so long and so complicated. Finally she came to a list of standard commands. She was pleased to see she had already mastered some of these – or rather guessed – such as saying 'LIGHT' to make the lights come on. It also said that when the System Administrator says aloud or writes on the wall the name of an item held within the C-Bean's Virtual Storage System, this enables the item to be retrieved through a Temporary Collection Portal. I know all about that, mused Alice, but what about when you just think it? The glass of water had appeared before she said a word about being thirsty. The manual went on: 'After the Access Panel has been activated for the first time using the Cardkey, the C-Bean may be voice activated to allow subsequent access. The C-Bean will remain programmed to respond only to the voice it was exposed to during the Imprinting Stage. This voice is the System Administrator.'

'Cool! So it was my voice the C-Bean was imprinted with that first day on the beach,' Alice murmured. 'But I still don't get how the transport function works …'

She flicked ahead in the manual. Page 99 described the use of the walls as interactive whiteboards (as she had guessed, they all worked as whiteboards). Finally, on page 100, Alice found what she was looking for: it said 'The C-Bean uses geo-stationary satellites to locate a destination on earth to a high degree of accuracy, but to ensure transportation to within a five-metre radius, precise north-south and east-west coordinates must be provided.' It also said, 'The coordinates may be inputted in "voice recognition mode" or in "script recognition mode"'.

Suddenly it all made sense: when she had written up the longitude and latitude coordinates of St Kilda on the wall it had transported the C-Bean to that location. Dr Foster must have remembered them ever so slightly wrong, and that was why they'd arrived out in the bay instead of on dry land.

The following day, Dr Foster promised the children that if they worked hard all morning, they could go in the C-Bean after lunch. Needless to say, they earned their time in the C-Bean. Alice led the way inside. The day before Dr Foster had suggested that, as the C-Bean was so empty inside, the children should bring in some of their own things. He suggested they could make a colour table each week, and put all sorts of things on it that were the same colour. This week's colour was red, so there in the middle of the resource table he'd put a large red apple, only it wasn't a real apple, it was too perfect and shiny. Dr Foster asked the children to gather round. Alice handed the instruction manual back to her teacher.

'Now, before Alice tells us all about what it says in the instruction manual, has anyone else brought something red for our collection?'

Sam J pulled his fire engine out of a plastic bag and put it next to the apple.

'Now that's impressive, son, and d'you know something?'

'What?' Sam asked.

'I happen to have ridden in a real fire engine exactly like this one.'

Sam was all ears.

'You see where it says NYC on the front? That stands for New York City – where I come from. That's why I brought the red apple: the nickname for my city is The Big Apple. And just along the street from where I used to live, there was a Fire Station, with a truck just like this one parked out front. One day we took the children I was teaching to meet the firemen and have a ride in it.' He nodded his head repeatedly after he said this.

Alice tried to imagine Dr Foster in his grey duffel coat walking down the street in a faraway place called The Big Apple, and seeing the red fire engine gleaming in the sunshine. It seemed so far away from St Kilda, just like Charlie's photo of Hong Kong.

Or was it? Alice felt a ripple of excitement in the pit of her stomach as she remembered the bit she'd read about the transport function. What if … ?

'Dr Foster, what longitude and latitude is New York?' she asked.

'Ah, that's a good question, Alice. Well it's a lot further west than here, and a bit further south too.'

'But where is New York exactly?' Alice persisted.

'Gee, we'd need to look it up …' Dr Foster began, and as he spoke the resource table began to flash with maps, starting with a satellite image of the Earth, and then zooming in and becoming more and more detailed, until the table was covered with a huge map showing a long green rectangle with patches of blue here and there.

'Well, would you believe it?' Dr Foster exclaimed. 'I think this is a map of Central Park, which is smack in the middle of New York.' He started to point out where the zoo and the skating rink were, and every time Dr Foster touched the map, the exact coordinates came up in a box.

'Aha, how interesting!' Dr Foster put his finger on a spot near the bottom of the long green rectangle, just beside one of the ponds. 'Now, here's the answer to your question Alice: 40 degrees, 46 minutes and 55 seconds North and 73 degrees, 57 minutes and 58 seconds West. Fancy that!'

Alice repeated the coordinates slowly under her breath. She couldn't be sure, but it was as if the C-Bean moved slightly. Dr Foster stood up to get a better look at the overall map, and as he stepped backwards, he seemed to fade out a little. His white hair and grey coat became paler and began to merge with the white wall behind him, until all Alice could see were his fluorescent yellow shoelaces. The children fell silent as their teacher drifted out of sight. Gradually they started to hear sounds, including something like the foghorn on the St Kilda ferry, only the booming came in short intermittent stabs. There were some voices in the distance, delicate birdsong, and then a siren, noisy and urgent.

'What shall we do?' asked Edie, searching Alice's face for answers.

'Go after him,' Alice said, peering eagerly into the misty white space. 'I have a feeling we're somewhere else.'

Sam J and Sam F stepped into the fog, their arms extended in front of them as if they were pretending to be zombies. Alice and Edie took hold of Hannah's hands, and followed after them. At first they thought they were surrounded by people, but in the misty gloom they saw that the C-Bean had arrived in the middle of a clump of trees. Dr Foster was sitting on the ground looking completely stunned and rubbing his forehead.

'Dr Foster, are you OK?' Alice enquired.

'Yes, I bumped my head on one of the trees, that's all.'

'Trees?' said Sam F. 'But there aren't any on our island!'

'We're not in St Kilda now, Sam,' said Alice quietly, looking at Dr Foster to see if he had any idea where he was.

'Then where are we?' said Edie irritably. 'I can't bear the way the C-Bean does this!'

Dr Foster got to his feet, and took charge.

'Kids, stay close to me. I'll find out what is going on.'

He moved out of the trees onto a narrow path that ran alongside them. The children followed close behind him. Alice looked back and saw the C-Bean standing blacker than ever as a ray of winter sunshine struggled between the bare branches of the trees. In the distance she could see the tops of buildings many times taller than the tallest tree.

'This is extraordinary!' said Dr Foster as they approached a large pond. 'We seem to be in the middle of Central Park ...' He fell silent for a moment or two, taking in his familiar surroundings. A smile crept across his face and he turned to face the children.

'Well, today it seems we're on a very special outing. Now kids, I want you to listen carefully. This might not be a real place at all, it might just be an illusion recreated from the C-Bean's memory bank, but I'm not taking any chances. None of you has been to a big city like this before, and it's very easy to get lost. But there's no point in not doing a couple of things before we go back to the C-Bean. Who wants to go to a real museum?'

The children clamoured 'Yes, me, yes please!'

'And afterwards we'll go to my favourite diner for a milkshake. Welcome to the Big Apple!' Dr Foster cleared his throat and said, 'This way, everyone.'

The park was full of people. They were walking dogs, pushing babies, drinking coffee, jogging, cycling or skating. Here and there snow had been heaped up beside the paths in dirty piles. A little brown dog joined them and started to trot along beside them as they moved around the edge of the frozen lake. They came to one edge of Central Park, and Alice could see a huge building up ahead. It had columns and steps and posters hanging down either side of the entrance. Above was a sign that said 'The American Museum of Natural History'.

Dr Foster stopped in front of it on the opposite side of the road and looked puzzled. 'Well for some reason it looks closed – let's see, it's Thursday lunchtime, now why would that be I wonder? Kids, wait here while I ask someone. Perhaps it's closed Thursdays.'

He crossed the road and spoke to a girl sitting on the museum steps. Alice could see Dr Foster looking at his watch and asking questions. The boys were marvelling at the constant stream of traffic that passed: cars, buses, yellow taxis and green trams with complicated overhead cables. Edie stood holding Hannah's hand and biting her lip. The little brown dog was sitting at Alice's feet, and she bent down to stroke it.

'Look Edie, Hannah, it's a lost dog.'

Finally their teacher rushed back over the road, smiling as though someone had told him a funny joke.

'Well it's quite simple,' he said, a little out of breath. 'I don't know why I didn't think of it: in St Kilda it's already lunchtime, but of course here in New York it's five hours behind, so in fact it's only eight o'clock in the morning. I'm afraid it's still breakfast time kids, and the museum doesn't open until nine.'

'Wicked! So can we have breakfast again?' Sam J chirped.

'Good thinking, Samuel! Let's go get ourselves an all-American breakfast, and when we're done, we can come back and look around.'

Dr Foster steered the five children up the next side street until they came to a big wide road called Broadway. Alice looked at all the apartment blocks, with their brown stone steps and metal fire escapes. There were all kinds of cooking and laundry smells coming from the houses. When they turned the corner into Broadway, Alice could see people with briefcases disappearing down steps that went under the pavement, and on every street corner there were flower stalls and newsstands. She tried to keep up with the others, but kept lagging behind, and a little voice trilled in her head again and again, 'You're in New York! You're in America!' It still seemed quite impossible that they really were being marched along a totally foreign street that was somehow quite familiar to their teacher.

Dr Foster stopped outside a small, friendly-looking cafe with seats inside covered in red plastic.

'This is the place, children. I hope you're feeling hungry!' He led them inside, and chose a table in a booth. They slid into their seats and a friendly-looking waitress called Cindy (according to her name badge) came over with six menus and a mug of coffee for Dr Foster.

The waitress explained all the choices on the menu, which went on for four pages, then left them to decide what they wanted. The pub on St Kilda only served jacket potatoes, with three different kinds of filling to choose from, and they'd never heard of half the things on offer: grits and scrapple didn't sound very nice, but waffles and syrup and Key Lime Pie for breakfast sounded delicious. The children took a long time asking Dr Foster's advice and comparing notes. Finally, the waitress took their order and the menus disappeared.

Alice noticed a machine on the table with words written on little pieces of card inside.

'Dr Foster, what's that?'

'Ah, that's a very old jukebox. If we put in a dime, it plays music. Shall we have a go?' Dr Foster fumbled in his pocket and, among his loose change, found the right coin. They chose a song called 'New York, New York'. Sam F pushed the buttons, and the machine sprang into life. After a minute, they were all singing along, even Edie, who was starting to look as though today's adventure might not be so bad after all.

When they'd eaten all the eggs, bacon, pancakes, muffins and maple syrup they could manage and Dr Foster had paid for it all with his credit card, they walked off down the street in high spirits. Alice checked her watch: it was almost two o'clock in St Kilda time, so take away five, that made it now just coming up to nine o'clock in New York.

Sure enough, the huge entrance doors to the museum were already open when they arrived back, and they clambered up the steps. Dr Foster got a map for each of them, and they stood in a circle to make a plan. Alice saw a poster advertising a new 3D film that was being shown at 11am about making energy from the waves.

'Look, Dr Foster, can we go and watch that?'

'There are hundred of things to see here, kids. How about we split up? I'm going to take Hannah and the boys, but Edie and Alice, you can look round by yourselves if you like.' He looked at his watch, 'So long as you meet me back here at, let's say, three … Oh …' Dr Foster stopped mid-sentence, and a look of dismay came across his face.

'I'm sorry to disappoint you kids, but I don't think we're going to have much time to look round the museum after all – your parents will be wondering where on earth we are if we don't get back in time for when school finishes. So in fact we only have about an hour.' He paused, and looked at their downcast faces.

'But we do have enough time to visit my favourite room. This way!'

Dr Foster led them briskly down the hall, through a hot sticky rainforest exhibit where they could hear the sound of tropical birds and insects, and into a small circular room containing a large display cabinet with a sign that said 'The drifting ocean currents'. Inside it were rows and rows of different shaped seabeans, each one polished by its journey across the ocean. They were round, fat, long, brown, red, grey and yellow. Alice could see hamburger seeds like the ones Dr Foster had given them, and a Mary's Bean like the one she'd given her mother. There were others called 'nicker nuts', 'sea purses', 'the snuff box sea bean' and the 'coco de mer'. Some of them had been made into necklaces and bracelets. There was a map showing where the seabeans had drifted from – Africa, Asia, America and Australia.

'Ours are way better,' Sam J concluded, grinning at his teacher. 'So what's next, Dr Foster?'

They looked round a few more exhibits they didn't quite understand, called things like 'The Polluted Planet', 'Magnetic Reversal' and 'Rising Sea Level'. They even had a quick look at something Alice spotted about nuclear versus wave energy, then the children were ushered back out onto the street again, where the little brown dog appeared to be waiting for them. They all stood waiting for a gap in the traffic to cross over to Central Park, chattering to each other about what they'd seen.

'I don't get it, Dr Foster, why is the sea level rising, and what was all that stuff about how the Earth's magnetism can switch over?' Edie asked.

A loud siren, which seemed to come from nowhere, abruptly drowned out Dr Foster's reply and they all looked round. A fire engine hurtled past them, exactly like Sam J's toy one.

'Wow!' exclaimed both boys, staring after it.

'Well, we've seen all the important things now,' chuckled Dr Foster. 'Let's get back to the C-Bean, quick as we can. It's a quarter after three in St Kilda.'

They crossed the road and the children started to run back to the little clump of trees where they'd left the C-Bean. As they approached, they could see a group of people had gathered around it, and some kind of smoke or mist seemed to be rising from the C-Bean. Alice saw a look of panic came over Dr Foster's face, and it occurred to her in a flash that perhaps the C-Bean was heading back to St Kilda without them.

The children made their way through the crowd of people and found the C-Bean being hosed down by three firemen wearing large yellow hats.

The same fire engine that they'd just seen go past had pulled up on the grass behind the trees.

'What are you guys doing?' Dr Foster asked the firemen, his voice sounding peculiarly mechanical all of a sudden.

'Someone reported a kiosk on fire in the Park. Is it yours, sir?'

'Yes. Yes it is.'

Hannah whispered to her sister, 'Someone's been drawing on the side of the C-Bean – look Edie.'

Across the whole of one surface, painted in angry spiky writing, someone had written 'Hadron burn in Hell!', with a background of cartoon-like flames in red and orange.

The firemen turned off the hose. Oddly enough, the C-Bean was not the slightest bit wet after its drenching, but there was no more smoke as far as Alice could tell, just the graffiti. People started to drift away now that the spectacle appeared to be over. Alice walked round to inspect the other sides of the C-Bean. She stood in front of the C-Bean's door, and whispered 'hello', then beckoned to the others as the door swung open, and everyone went inside. Everyone, that is, except Dr Foster. Alice went back out to look for him.

Dr Foster was holding a piece of paper in his hand and was talking to a man in uniform. Alice could only hear snippets of their conversation: 'No, we don't have a permit to locate here … Today … Yes, I realise that … What? A hundred dollar fine!' The little brown dog was circling round Alice's legs. It wagged its tail and barked at her. The man in uniform looked across, frowning.

Alice waved to catch Dr Foster's attention, and Dr Foster said, 'Excuse me for a moment, sir,' and then hurried across to the C-Bean. Alice pulled her teacher inside and clicked the door shut. Then she said loudly and forcefully, 'Where is ST KILDA? Where is a PEN?' Within moments, satellite maps illuminated the central table. Alice touched on the map to enlarge Village Bay, and then touched the spot behind the church where their schoolyard lay.

Alice grabbed the pen as soon as it appeared in the collection portal. As Edie called out the exact coordinates, Alice wrote them onto the white wall.

There was a pause. The children were utterly silent, each holding their breath, willing the C-Bean to return home and quickly. In the silence, they could hear a strange snuffling sound. There was a slight jolt and the door opened. Dr Foster's red plastic apple rolled off the table and out through the door, chased by a little brown dog.

Chapter 6: Cloud Forest

The little dog shook itself dry and looked around the schoolyard. The door into the school had been left open, and he trotted inside into the warmth. The children's empty sandwich boxes were on their desks, and the dog sniffed each of them in turn, licking up crumbs. Obviously rather hungry, he went over to Dr Foster's desk where he found an open packet of biscuits. The dog tugged at the wrapping and two digestives fell out, sprinkling a shower of crumbs onto his fur. The dog was just licking his chops contentedly when the first child appeared.

Sam F caught sight of something scuttling away when he entered the classroom. Whatever it was ran and hid under the nature table. He thought perhaps it was one of the St Kilda mice, which sometimes came inside on a cold winter's day and were twice the size of a normal mouse. Having seen so many incredible things that day, he didn't give it another thought.

Dr Foster stood beside the C-Bean and made sure all the children emerged safely, and then followed them back into the schoolroom. He was still holding the hundred dollar fine he'd been issued. Alice saw him stare at it again, raise his eyebrows and shake his head as he walked back to his desk. Then he screwed it up and threw it in the recycling bin.

'Well, kids, it's been quite an unbelievable day. Literally. I bet we'll all wake up tomorrow and think it was some kind of weird dream. I think we've discovered that the C-Bean has immense powers, and if we treat it well, there might be other journeys it will take us on. I'm just glad that the first one happened to be somewhere I know!'

'Can we go on another adventure tomorrow?' Sam J piped up hopefully.

'Not until I've read the instruction manual properly, no. I'm sorry we didn't have time for you to give us the proper tour today, Alice, but I think in the circumstances I'd better have a good read of it myself this evening. See you tomorrow everyone.'

Alice stayed behind to email Charlie. She needed to share her experience with someone.

Charlie – Our new classroom called the C-Bean is absolutely amazing. I can't wait for you to come back. Today it took us to New York – really! Alice.

As she shut down the computer, she heard a scuffling noise, and then she felt something warm and wet nudge her hand. When she looked round there was the little dog, sitting quietly on the story rug behind her, his head tilted on one side.

'Oh, it's you. You're definitely lost now! Come here, little one.'

The dog shuffled forwards on his bottom, then stopped and wagged his tail. She could hear a low chuckling bark grow in the back of the dog's throat. When he woofed the sound echoed around the high ceiling of the old school room, and the dog appeared to frighten himself. Alice ruffled his fur.

'Well I can't leave you here,' she said. 'You'll have to come home with me.'

The two of them sauntered up the grassy street in the twilight, the dog weaving from side to side as it caught new smells, but always returning to Alice's side. The seabirds were calling above the cliffs in the distance. There were no other dogs on the island, apart from the dog that belonged to one of the men who worked on the ferry. This one was quite similar – the same kind of mixed-up mongrel – only he had no collar and apparently no name. A waif and stray that had accidentally found its way from New York to St Kilda. Alice could not imagine what her parents would say.

'Wait here,' she told the dog, and he sat down by the back door.

Alice went in. Her mum was feeding Kit on the sofa. She snuggled up beside them. She was about to tell her mother about the dog, when he appeared in front of them, uttered a soulful little cry, and lay down. Alice's mum jumped, and the baby started to cry.

'Mum, it's OK, don't be scared. This is our new dog, he just got here, and he's called …' – Alice cast her eye around the room looking for inspiration – 'he's called Spex,' she decided, as her eyes landed on her mum's glasses case.

Alice's mum was rocking Kit to stop him crying. She didn't look cross, but she didn't look pleased either.

'Is that so? Is that because he ex-Spex to be looked after?' her mother teased. 'Is he the ferryman's dog?' She paused but Alice didn't answer her. She just tried to look appealing. Taking his cue from Alice, the dog was trying to look appealing too, with his head on one side. Alice's mum laughed.

'Well, it's OK by me for you to have a new friend, but you'll have to ask Dad what he thinks too.'

'Where is Daddy?'

'Down at the shed. He'll be back later. He said he needed to work late this evening.'

Alice took the dog into the kitchen and gave him some leftover porridge in a bowl. Then she scrunched up an old blanket and put it next to the row of wellies.

'C'mon Spex!' she said, trying out the new name and patting the bed.

The dog climbed obediently into the bed. Tomorrow she would ask Mrs Butterfield to order in some dog food from the mainland. Over breakfast she would try and convince Dad about keeping Spex.

It rained all night, hard thundering drops plummeting down so fast they sounded like they were making craters in the thick turf roof above Alice's bed. It rained so hard she could not help dreaming of rain. They were sheltering under some trees in Central Park, only the trees were closing in, and she saw they were actually policemen encircling her, and she couldn't get past them to look for the C-Bean. Everything was a blur of green uniforms and green leaves, all pressing into her face, brushing past her with their wet surfaces … Spex was licking her hand, and Alice woke up.

The dog stared at her sleepy face, barked and ran round in circles, begging her to get up. She looked at her alarm clock: 7.30 am. Alice pulled on her dressing gown and wellies and went down the passage to open up the back door and let the dog out. It was still dark and still raining, but the little dog didn't seem to mind, and ran off sniffing at tussocks of grass and lapping up puddles. Alice laughed and ran after the dog, splashing in the puddles. Spex disappeared into one of the stone storehouses and reappeared dragging a long stick. Alice threw it for him to fetch a few times and then called him back to the house.

'We've got a dog!' she said out loud suddenly. 'Spex, you're coming to school with me. You are officially our school pet. Come on.'

When she got to school the others were already inside the C-Bean, drawing and writing with the digital pens on the table. Dr Foster had asked them to make a record of what they'd seen the day before in New York, and left them to get on while he went to make an urgent phone call. Everything they wrote or drew on the table, the C-Bean seemed to be storing and making into a big display up on the walls around them.

Alice was late because she had been looking for something to use as a dog lead. Spex had obviously never been put on a lead before, and didn't much like the feel of the long scarf she'd tied round his neck, so it had been quite a struggle. The dog walked round the C-Bean trailing his homemade lead and wagging his tail happily as all the children patted him.

Alice said, 'Meet Spex, everyone. He escaped from New York just like Dr Foster!' Then she made him sit beside her at the table. She watched the others working quietly for a while, a whole blank expanse of table in front of her waiting for her to begin too.

All she could think about were the dense green trees in her dream. Alice stared down at the table and watched as the outlines of branches began to appear, each one growing more and more twigs, overlapping and making complex patterns. It looked like shadows on a forest floor, all moving slightly. Soon the whole table was covered with her interlocking branches and twigs.

'Hey, what's going on?' Sam F rubbed the table with his arm, trying to get rid of the branches that were starting to obscure what he was doing. He picked up his bag from the floor, pulled out his lunch box and his walkie-talkie set and dropped them onto the table, then rooted around inside to find something to try to clean the table with. The noise broke Edie's and Sam J's concentration and they looked up. Hannah was drawing skyscrapers on her side of the table, and had not yet noticed the spreading tree pattern.

Alice stood up. The air in the C-Bean had become warm and steamy as the children's breath mingled with the moisture coming off their damp clothes. The branches were not just on the table, they were appearing above the table too, faint fragments of twisting lengths of bark, then as the holograms grew, vines with huge fleshy flowers and fruits hanging down began to appear. The holograms became stronger and darker, filling up the whole space inside the C-Bean now, so that Alice could hardly see the surrounding walls any more. Spex tugged on his lead and trotted off, his nose close to the ground.

'Spex, wait!' Sam F called, as he tried to grab him, missed, and chased after him. Alice watched as they both disappeared behind a thick clump of trees.

'Edie, Sam, Hannah. Quick – it's happened again! Sam and Spex have gone.'

She stuffed the things back into Sam F's bag, slung it over her shoulder and followed after them.

The children fell into single file behind Spex, moving quickly between the trees in silence. The mist clung to the trees and was even thicker above their heads as they picked their way through the tangled green undergrowth. Alice could hear croaking and squawking from all directions. It was suffocatingly hot and sticky, like when you have been standing in a very hot shower and can hardly breathe because the air is so full of tiny drops of water. Within minutes the children were peeling off their sweaters and tying them round their waists. But they kept on moving.

After a while, the trees starting to thin out, and they found themselves at the edge of a huge empty clearing covered in yellow earth. Sam F stopped abruptly and turned round.

'Where are we? This isn't Central Park is it, like yesterday?' His eyes were wide and sweat was dripping off his chin.

Alice looked around the clearing and realised there were tree stumps dotted everywhere, each one sticking a short way out of the ground. It looked as if they had recently been chopped down. Along one side of the clearing she could see something large and bright green, and behind it a wall of sheer rock. She could hear someone shouting and their echo bouncing off the rock.

'I think we should keep a low profile until we work out where we are,'

Alice said quietly. 'Let's watch what's going on from behind those bushes over there.'

Edie looked doubtful. 'I think we should just go back to the C-Bean,' she said.

'No way!' said Sam J. 'This place is like a proper jungle. I bet there are monkeys and everything.'

'And what about those bats that drink nectar, the ones Dr Foster told us about! I saw one of those weird seedpods on a tree back there,' added Sam F.

'Hannah, what do you think?' Alice asked.

Hannah sniffed and looked at Edie, who was standing with her arms folded. She was wearing green flowery leggings that blended into the background and made her look like she belonged in a rainforest.

'I like it here,' she said, 'it smells nice.'

'What will happen if one of us gets lost or hurt or something? What if we get kidnapped, and never get back to St Kilda?' Edie protested, but she knew the others had won. 'OK, but we have to stick together. No one runs off, right?'

The children nodded. Suddenly they heard a sound like a gunshot, and then its echo a moment later. An engine fired up, and the green thing on the far side of the clearing began to move. As it moved out into the sunlight Alice could see it was a tractor with long caterpillar tracks. It was making its way towards them. Without saying a word, the children ran behind the bushes and crouched down.

Spex meanwhile had wandered off and was standing right out in the open when he saw the huge green vehicle approaching. He began to bark. The barks volleyed back to him so loudly off the rock that he must have thought there was another dog, and he stopped, pricked up his ears, and then lay low with his belly pressed to the ground. The children gulped and held their breath, crouching lower.

The vehicle stopped and a man jumped down. He had a dark face and was wearing a yellow baseball cap and dirty overalls the same green as the caterpillar tractor. He pulled off the cap and wiped his forehead, then pulled it back on. He stood still for a moment watching Spex and, as he started to move towards him, his hand reached into his pocket.

Alice saw a flash of metal and was convinced it was a gun, but the man brought it up to his mouth to drink. By the time he put the flask back in his pocket, Spex had slunk away.

The man climbed back behind the wheel again, and turned the vehicle round on the soft yellow earth. The tracks churned up the surface behind it, and blobs of silvery liquid trickled into all the ruts. At first Alice thought it was petrol. It definitely wasn't water. The thought of the water made Alice realise how thirsty she was.

The children waited until the tractor disappeared, and began walking in the opposite direction in search of water. When they reached the rock, Alice remembered Sam's bag and brought out his lunchbox. They shared out the ham sandwiches (Hannah didn't want one) and the carton of apple juice between them, and each had a bite of his apple.

They could hear a constant loud hissing sound in the distance. A bit further on they came across some equipment where the caterpillar tractor had been parked. There was a stack of shallow metal pans, all dented and smeared with the yellow earth, a couple of metal cylinders and several reels of hosepipe.

'Must be water near here somewhere if there's a hosepipe,' remarked Sam F, picking an apple pip out of his teeth.

'Whoa!' shouted Sam J in a choked voice, and Alice could see a look of fear creeping over his face.

They walked to Sam J. He threw his arms out to stop them as they reached him and they saw that one step further on was a sheer drop, taller than any cliff face on St Kilda. Spread out below them was a kind of quarry, with hundreds of workers moving mounds of yellow rock using machinery while others were hosing down piles of rock. The children hadn't heard the sound of the mine because the quarry lay at the edge of a huge cascading waterfall. The hissing sound they'd been hearing had turned into a ferocious roar, louder than the roughest waves that ravaged Village Bay in winter.

Alice's legs were shaking as they all moved back from the cliff edge. When they turned round, they could see the caterpillar tractor returning. There was nowhere to hide this time, so they began to run for cover in the trees on the nearest edge of the clearing. Their feet slid in the yellow mud, and with every step across the clearing more and more lumps of it stuck to the bottoms of their shoes.

'Hey!' a voice shouted. Alice tried to go faster, but the others were much further ahead. She could see Sam F at the back, his bag hanging open, as he tried to keep up with the rest. She saw something fall out of the bag into the mud. She looked back and could see two men coming after them. She stumbled on. The men were shouting again. She saw something black and silver in the mud – it was one half of Sam's walkie-talkie. She picked it up, and spotted a boulder up ahead. Breathing hard, she hid herself behind the boulder and waited. The shouting stopped, and all she could hear was the distant roar of the waterfall.

Alice closed her eyes and counted to a hundred. Then she half-stood and peeped over the top of the boulder. In the mist she could see the caterpillar tractor moving off and a group of men following behind it, carrying their equipment. She could just make out a name written on the side of the truck: *Eldorado Brasil*. She saw one of the men lean over the cliff edge and signal something down to the people in the mine below. He was pointing in her direction. She felt sweat rolling down her back. Another trickle ran into her eye and she could feel its salty sting.

She waited a minute longer, and then called out 'Edie? Sam? Wait for me!'

There was no sign of the others. She scrambled through the undergrowth, and realised she had no idea where she was going, or which direction the C-Bean was. She was still holding the walkie-talkie in her hand and, with fingers crossed, she switched it on.

'Hello. Come in Sam! Are you there Sam? ANSWER ME!'

But there was no reply, just a soft crackle. Now she couldn't tell if it was sweat or tears in her eyes. She stumbled and caught her knee on a thorny vine lying coiled on the ground and disturbed some creatures up above. There was a loud squawking and she saw a flash of vivid blue further ahead. Her knee was bleeding, but she just rubbed it and continued walking.

There was a pile of blue feathers on the path ahead of her. The trees were very close together now and the forest was quite dark, but Alice could make out something moving under the feathers. She put the walkie-talkie down and crept forwards very slowly.

A large bird was clawing the air with its black scaly legs, trying to stand upright. Alice bent down and smoothed its feathers, but she was afraid of lifting the bird because it had a very sharp-looking beak. The bird eyed her with its bright yellow eye, tilted its head, and squawked. She decided it must be some kind of parrot.

'Hello,' Alice said.

'*Olá*,' answered the bird.

The bird managed to stand upright and began a sort of lopsided hopping. Alice laughed. It was showing off she thought, splaying out its tail feathers, organising them with its beak, and chanting '*Olá olá!*'

The walkie-talkie made a tapping sound, then a voice crackled, 'Alice, is that you?'

Alice grabbed the walkie-talkie and fumbled with the button on the side, pressing it and speaking into the mouthpiece.

'Edie, is that you?'

'Negative. It's Sam Fitzpatrick.'

'Thank goodness! That wasn't me, Sam, it was a parrot you heard.'

'Did you say a carrot?'

'Where are you Sam? Have you got back to the C-Bean yet?'

'Negative.'

'Is everyone with you?'

'Affirm … yes.'

'Including Spex?'

'Yup. He's here.'

'Tell him to come and find me Sam.'

'How do I do that? He's a dog.'

'I know, but just try. Say, "go find Alice" or something.'

'OK.'

'Keep this thing on, OK?'

Alice stroked the bird's feathers and waited. Her knee was throbbing now and her throat felt like it was coated with sandpaper. After a moment or two the parrot clambered onto her lap, and then hopped up onto her shoulder. He was using his beak and his claw to open a seed. She watched as he managed to open the seedpod and then remove the seeds. She wasn't sure if she should keep moving or not.

Suddenly the little dog bounded through the undergrowth and ran round Alice, wagging and barking. The parrot flew up into a branch in alarm and squawked loudly.

'Spex!' Alice was so relieved to see him she felt sick and cold all of a sudden. He licked her face and sat at her feet, looking very pleased with himself.

'Where are the others, Spex?' she asked, shivering.

The dog started sniffing the ground and rooting in the undergrowth. He picked up the walkie-talkie in his mouth and brought it to her. As Alice put her cardigan back on she felt the other card key to the C-Bean in her pocket. She studied the silvery image of the earth and ran her fingers over the writing on the front.

How were they going to find the C-Bean again? Why had it come to this place when no one had written any coordinates on the wall?

The bird squawked at Spex, and flew into the next tree. Spex jumped up and barked, then ran further along the path the way he'd come. Alice followed, and the parrot flew down, its feathers still dishevelled. She stopped and realised it was slightly injured.

'C'mon, hop on,' she said gently, holding her arm out. The scaly legs gripped onto the sleeve of her cardigan, and she found she could only walk quite slowly with the parrot. The dog ran back from time to time, leading the way. At one point they had to wade across a narrow stream. Spex splashed across. And back again. Alice thought about taking off her shoes and socks, but then thought it was safer to keep them on in case there was anything in the water that could bite or sting her. She moved through the shallowest part as quickly as she could, the parrot still clinging to her left shoulder.

Up ahead, there were more and more trees and the path disappeared from time to time. They had to push their way through the tangle of undergrowth. The bird flew up into the branches, and limped from one tree to another. Just when Alice had no idea which direction she should be heading, the walkie-talkie made a bleeping noise. Alice tried to speak into it, but there was no reply. It wasn't even crackling now. The batteries must have gone dead. She felt as if she might cry at any moment. She swallowed hard. All she had now was the card key. She took it out of her pocket and held it up to the light again. Something had changed. The globe was spinning very slowly. Alice remembered how when she first found it, the globe spun faster when she approached the slot. What if …

Alice moved more quickly now, ignoring Spex and the parrot. After a few metres the globe stopped spinning. She stopped, turned, and set off in the opposite direction. A few moments later the globe started rotating again. She pressed on, and the rotations got a little faster. Alice's heartbeat sounded louder than the roar of the waterfall now. She couldn't hear the dog barking or the parrot squawking, and she could no longer feel the pain in her knee. Just keep going, she told herself, the spinning globe will show me the way.

Alice's Blog #3

28th January 2018

You know I'm really supposed to be writing about life on this island for my blogs, but it seems that lately we've been spending a lot of time getting stuck in other places, so I don't think this is really going to make much sense to some people reading it. I mean, who's going to believe it when I write about us popping over to New York for the afternoon, or the Amazon rainforest for a couple of hours?

So if you think I'm making it up, whoever you are reading this, it's up to you. By the way, you can post me a message telling me what you think on this website and I can have a look. And if anyone out there knows anything about a C-Bean Mark 3, or has one too, our teacher Dr Foster would really like to talk to you. It had him really worried the last time. He only went back inside the school to make a phone call, and after that the door to the C-Bean wouldn't open. Apparently we were gone for over two hours. To me it seemed like much longer, but then I was totally lost in the middle of a rainforest with a poorly knee, a stray dog and an injured bird, being chased by some men with a caterpillar tractor and not knowing where on earth the others were, let alone the C-Bean.

But when I found the other cardkey in my pocket, I just knew I could find my way back. I beat the others to the C-Bean by five minutes and thirty seconds in the end. I could tell that Edie had been crying because she was frowning and sniffing and wouldn't even look at me when they arrived back, but she didn't say anything because they had too much to tell me.

The boys were so excited they could only explain things with actions and sound effects. They jumped around with their arms near their knees whooping until I got the general idea about the monkeys they'd seen. Then their arms started juddering back and forth and they made a buzzing noise through their teeth as they described how they'd watched some more trees being cut down with chainsaws. But when they got to the last part, both Sams fell silent and let Edie open Sam F's bag and reach inside.

I knew it wasn't an animal because she would be too scared to do that kind of thing. If one of the boys had reached inside the bag, I would have guessed a tree frog or a huge furry spider, or one of the bats they'd been talking about. But it was much more beautiful. Edie stood in a little patch of sunlight, pulled out a large lump of something she'd wrapped up in some tissues, and held out her hands for me to see.

It was knobbly, like a giant piece of popcorn when it's got stuck together with sugar at the bottom of the bowl. Only it was more yellow, and it looked hard like play-dough when it's been left out too long. Except it shone.

Both Sams clamoured, 'Can you guess what it is?'

I was looking at a huge lump of solid gold. Edie said they found it half buried next to a metal pan like the ones we'd seen earlier in the clearing. It was as if someone was trying to hide it and then maybe had run off, and was too scared to come back for it. When Edie gave it to me it was so heavy I had to use both hands to hold it. Sam J said he knew it was real gold because he had bitten it, like pirates do, to test it's not fake, and he showed me the teeth marks.

Then it was my turn. Spex was still snuffling round my feet, so the parrot stayed stubbornly up in the tree until I got Hannah to hold the dog still. I called to the bird, and there was a flash of bright blue and then he landed on my arm. I said, 'Say hello to my friends', and it was like we'd been rehearsing it all the way through the forest, because he said 'Olá' to them, and even did a little bow with his head. Everyone laughed, which made him embarrassed, so he started fiddling with his broken tail feathers.

But that was just the beginning of the Show and Tell session: when we got inside the C-Bean, it had its own story to tell. It started showing us all kinds of data on the walls, including maps and photos of everywhere we'd just been, of the men and the quarry and loads of close ups of all the equipment. I noticed that we were even in some of the pictures. The notes and images were being put into some sort of sequence on the central table, and we could see the yellow earth, and the caterpillar tracks, and Sam's walkie-talkie lying on the ground in one.

Then the C-Bean started to label everything it had photographed: it put words like 'gold panning equipment', 'mercury amalgamation process' and 'cyanidation', whatever that is. I got the feeling they must be all be about something dangerous or polluting because the words flashed red and a yellow triangular warning sign came up beside them. I wanted to read everything to know what it all meant, but Edie was getting really worried about us getting back, so in the end we just wrote up the coordinates of St Kilda (I know them off by heart now) and waited for the little jolt to know we were back in the schoolyard. Just as I walked out of the door I remembered that the manual said the C-Bean was assembled in Brazil. Perhaps it was homesick.

We could see Dr Foster through the window, pacing up and down in the schoolroom. He kept running his hands through his white hair and making funny faces like someone had just stepped on his toe. He didn't even seem to hear us when we opened the door. We walked in quietly and sat down at our desks.

I can't remember what he said to us exactly last Friday. He didn't really even need to say anything. We thought he was going to shout at us for getting locked inside the C-Bean without permission. It seemed like he didn't know whether to be cross or pleased to see us. He kept starting sentences and then sighing and not finishing them. Some of the things he said were more to himself than to us, like 'I should have been there,' and 'It's just not fair'. It took us a long time to realise that he was not talking about our adventure at all, but something much more serious and upsetting.

The phone call that Dr Foster had to go and make earlier that morning was to New York. After he managed to tell us that, there was a long pause, and his eyes went very red. He blew his nose into a large white hanky, and smoothed his hair again. Then he said that there had been a fatal accident in his family. He told us his sister worked in a research laboratory where they did experiments using poisonous chemicals. I might have been imagining it, but I think he even used the word 'cyanide'. He said had to go back to New York. He had to get a plane. The helicopter was coming for him. He had to give her a decent funeral. He was sorry, but school would be closed for a few days.

Dr Foster never even noticed that there was a bright green parrot in the room who'd been listening very attentively all the way through, not even when our teacher stood up to leave and it did a sympathetic little squawk. I wanted to give Dr Foster a hug, but he just put on his big grey duffle coat, picked up his battered leather briefcase, smiled at us with sad eyes, and left. We all looked at each other, and had nothing to say. All I knew was I couldn't say the word 'dead' out loud.

Edie walked over to the nature table, took the golden nugget out of its tissue wrapper and put it carefully in the middle. Then she dried her eyes on one of the tissues and threw them all in the bin.

We found a jar of sunflower seeds in the classroom and gave them to our parrot. He was hopping from foot to foot with excitement as we fed them to him one by one. When the seeds were all gone, he started squawking 'Peri-gro-so, peri-gro-so'. I could tell the bird was getting upset about something. He flew over to the window and sat on the windowsill sulking. He was still there the next morning.

I asked my parents, do parrots sleep at night? What do they need to keep healthy and happy? These are things we are going to have to find out, because there are only seabirds on St Kilda for company, and he's not the same as them and I don't suppose he even speaks their language. Mum and Dad think I've been given a project to do on parrots while Dr Foster is away.

Dad says I can help him in the wave energy lab if I haven't got anything else to do next week. I said, only if there are no poisonous chemicals like cyanide in his lab. Then he gave me a lecture about how there are way too many poisons in the air we breathe and in the food we eat and the water we drink, and about all the heavy metals that are getting into our eco-systems and ruining our planet.

I said, 'What, like gold?' Dad said, 'Gold's not a heavy metal,' and I said, 'Yes it is, it's very heavy actually,' but he said it was just inert.

I asked him what inert meant, and he said, it means that you can eat it and it wouldn't do anything to your insides. But he said they use dangerous chemicals in the gold mines, like cyanide and mercury, to make the tiny bits of gold stick together. Dad said that mercury is heavy metal and, interestingly, it's also the only metal that's a liquid most of the time.

After he'd told me all that I said, 'Dad, you should be our replacement teacher while Dr Foster is away, you'd be quite good at it!' and he just laughed and said he was too busy.

I kept thinking about the silver liquid in the caterpillar tracks. Was that mercury? Did we find a gold mine?

Later that evening, I asked Mum if she had ever heard of Eldorado. She was singing Kit an old Scottish song she used to sing to me when I was little, so at first she didn't answer. I sat on the bed and waited until Kit was snoring softly in his cot, and then Mum put her arm round me and told me a story about a beautiful city where everything was made of gold. The mayor of the city covered himself with gold too, and they called him El Dorado, the golden man. Mum said she thought it was supposed to be somewhere up the Amazon in Peru or Brazil, but that no one had ever really found it. Then she said sleepily, 'Why do you ask?'

I wanted to blurt out, 'That proves it!' The lump we brought back really IS gold. And wherever we went to wasn't just anywhere, it was Eldorado. It exists. But they've ruined it. All the trees have been cut down. Instead I said, 'I saw the name written down somewhere, that's all.'

29th January 2018

Today was the first day of no school. I stared at the map of St Kilda that's on the wall in our kitchen while I ate my breakfast, wondering what to do. It's a really detailed old map with every little lump and bump marked in wiggly lines called contours. If you go across the lines you're walking uphill or downhill, and if you go along in between the lines, you are walking on a level. Only you can't see the lines in real life. Unless you're a mapmaker. I bet mapmakers walk around and see contours everywhere they go. On the cliffs, the lines are bunched so close together they're almost touching.

I tried to imagine that instead of being one or two miles across our little island was in fact a huge continent, and that the little stream running down towards the sea was actually a massive river like the Amazon. So I bet you can imagine how my heart skipped a beat when I saw a little black symbol marked Amazon's House on the Gleann Mor side of the island! I went up closer to have a better look. It said on the key at the side of the map, 'believed to be the hunting lodge of a fabled female warrior'. We walked all over the island the summer we moved here, but I don't remember seeing this house or hearing that name.

A plan exploded into my head. I ran round to Edie's with Spex and persuaded her and Hannah to come on an expedition to Gleann Mor. Jane, their mum, made us all a packed lunch, and we walked over to Sam J's house. Sam F was there too, and they were playing with the walkie-talkie set, which was working again now they'd put some new batteries in it. In the end, we all ate lunch there, and set off with our bellies full of soup and sandwiches. Mrs Jackson gave us some flapjacks wrapped in silver foil and a bottle of water to share between us.

It was spitting as we set off, and Spex darted around in between our legs, shaking himself dry every now and again but making us wetter. He seemed more excited about this adventure than the trek through a real rainforest, probably because he wasn't on the lead.

We followed the stream that runs into the Bay back to where it first appears out of the ground, just past the end of the village. There are stone cleits dotted all over this part of the valley, but they stop when the ground gets steeper. Dad told me once there are over a thousand of them on St Kilda. We could see the radar station spying on us from the summit. We climbed higher up until we were at the bit shaped like a saddle, where you can suddenly see the other side of the island. Well, if I'm honest, we only caught a tiny glimpse of the cove in the distance before the clouds closed in and it became too misty to see anything very much.

Hannah was soaked and shivery. She said she wanted to go back home, but we persuaded her to keep going. Edie and I held her hands and we ran down the other side, so she would warm up. Spex barked all the way down.

I was worried we'd miss the Amazon's House, but we nearly ran into it. It was about the same size and height as the C-Bean, but made out of long thin stones, and instead of a perfect cube, it was circular with a mossy dome on top. We walked around the walls until we found the way in.

'It stinks of dead sheep in here,' remarked Sam J, as he ran his hand along a ledge on the inside wall. The ledge turned into a deep shelf and he climbed up onto it. 'And bird poo.'

'Can we have a flapjack now?' Sam F asked. Edie opened the silver foil and we all helped ourselves, including Spex who ate the remaining crumbs as well. As our eyes adjusted to the gloom, we could see other shelves and cubbyholes built into the walls. Here and there stones were missing, and you could feel gusts of wind and rain coming through the cracks. I could see something that looked metallic in one of the cracks, and when I reached out to pick it up, there was a sound like a sword being pulled out of its scabbard. I asked the others if they could hear something like scraping metal, but they said they couldn't.

After the others had gone back outside, I examined the metallic thing. It was smaller than the C-Bean's cardkey, attached to a chain, and had rounded corners. It was dull and dirty, but when I rubbed off some of the dirt, I could see it said RAF and had a long number and some initials punched onto it: DCF.

In the stillness I could hear another noise, like a woman clearing her throat. Without saying a word, I put the metal thing on a chain back into the recess, zipped up my coat, and stood very still. It felt like someone was breathing just in front of me, and for some reason I imagined I was standing face to face with the female warrior who once lived here. I stared hard at the space in front of me. She didn't move or make a sound, but I could feel her warm hands touch my hair. I couldn't be sure but I think she also whispered Kit, Kit, Kit. It might have been a bird or the wind, of course. But whatever it was, it really made me shiver.

I ran outside. The others were down by the water where Spex was sniffing trails of scent. The sea in the cove looked strange – like it was burnt – and it moved in a sort of syrupy way.

When I got closer I could see that Spex was not sniffing but picking things up and carrying them and then putting them down again higher up the slope, away from the water. His tail was wagging with delight because he had found something that needed to be done, but when I saw what it was, I yelled at him to stop.

I counted a hundred birds. They were all different species – skuas, fulmars, petrels, guillemots, gannets, kittiwakes – all lying on top of each other, all dead. They'd been washed up by the last tide and stank of rotting fish. Their feathers were sticky with this thick black film. The boggy grass was covered in the same stuff, all the way up to the last high tide mark, where a long line of rubbish and seaweed had collected, all stuck together like treacle toffee.

The skies had cleared a bit. I looked out to the horizon. I'd heard about tankers that crashed into rocks and split open, spilling their cargoes of oil everywhere. I knew it had happened in other parts of Scotland before. But there were no ships in sight. We decided we needed to tell someone what we'd found, and we knew there would be someone up at the radar station we could tell. They could get a message to the mainland, and send someone over to investigate.

Halfway up the hill, the rain started again in earnest, and we were walking straight into it. I could feel it lashing my face, even with my hood pulled close against my cheeks. We lost sight of the radar station, and although we had Edie's compass we still couldn't work out which way we were walking. A soggy Spex followed me, his tail between his legs, waiting for me to show that I had forgiven him for moving the birds.

We never did find the radar station that day, but we did manage to make it back to Village Bay before it got dark.

In the local online newspaper it said that Mr McLintock called a meeting in the pub and five men hiked over to Gleann Mor the next morning. They could see for themselves that something had to be done about the damage the oil had caused. Everyone was angry, and a reporter arrived by helicopter from Glasgow with three environmental experts to work out what had happened. Dad says he's even more determined now we're not going to let the island be sold to those Russian oil people. But we haven't got much time. There was another piece on the website which said that the school was closed on St Kilda for the time being, because of a death in the teacher's family, and that he had returned to New York to attend his sister's funeral, who had died 'under suspicious circumstances'.

There seems to be altogether too much sadness here at the moment. Even our parrot is down in the dumps. I don't think he likes the cold, and he is definitely not a fan of peanuts. I got him some from the shop yesterday, but he seems to prefer pork scratchings.

2nd February 2018

It's been raining non-stop for three whole days. I've emailed Charlie in Hong Kong six times, but he hasn't replied. So I've decided to add some more to my blog.

The reporter told Dad last night that one of the environmentalists thinks the birds did not all die because of the oil slick. Instead they might have been poisoned by the fish they ate. So they've sent samples of the contents of their stomachs in test tubes on the ferry today, to be tested in a lab in Glasgow. We rang Lori there yesterday to wish her happy birthday, but she said she hadn't heard anything about all these catastrophes.

Today we did every jigsaw we have, including the one I got for my birthday, and then played every game we could think of. Edie won every time, and out of pure frustration, Sam J and Sam F had a big fight. The only thing I could think of to make them stop fighting was probably not such a great idea. I suggested, as Charlie was not replying to any of my emails, that we could, if we wanted to, pay him a visit.

Everyone went quiet and looked at each other. We knew school was meant to be off limits, but no one had said anything about the C-Bean. Just a short trip, I suggested, and we'd come straight back.

They didn't need much convincing. We've decided to do it tomorrow, while there's a special emergency meeting about the oil slick going on.

Chapter 7: Quicksilver

A strong smell of garlic drifted into the C-Bean, but even then the children had no way of knowing if it had worked or not. Once again, the walls had become cloudy and porous and all they needed to do was to walk through it to find out if they had arrived, and if so, where exactly.

'Well, are we going out or not?' For once, it was Edie who seemed impatient to find out. The others nodded. This time, they'd come prepared: Alice had left Spex at home that morning, she'd brought the C-Bean's instruction manual with her, and they'd all brought lunchboxes.

Even when they were out of the C-Bean, they still seemed to be in the middle of a cloud. In the far distance they could hear the hum of traffic and strange incantations that sounded like someone singing very out of tune through a loudspeaker. The sounds seemed to be coming from below. Alice thought they must have got Charlie's coordinates wrong, and that somehow they'd ended up in the sky. But then she realised she was walking on a kind of hard grey surface. She bumped into another wall that felt at first like the C-Bean, and heard someone else do the same.

'Hey, what's this? Did the C-Bean move?' Sam F demanded.

Alice knocked on the side of the other smooth flat-sided thing, and a deep metallic boom resonated and seemed to echo away down a long tunnel. Feeling her way around the side of the metallic object, it started to curve away and then she found a large rectangular opening. The cloud was thicker still around the opening.

'Hello!' Alice said very quietly, just to test it.

'*Olá!*' came the echo.

Then there was the unmistakeable sound of squawking and feathers flapping.

'Who brought the stupid parrot? I thought we agreed to leave him behind.' Edie's sense of adventure was vanishing already. But so too was the cloud, and the bird's blue shape slowly emerged from the billowing whiteness, silhouetted against a large silver air-conditioning duct.

'Hey, we're on top of a roof!' Sam F said suddenly, peering over the edge of the nearest ledge at the streets far below.

'Guys, this is not just any roof – we're on top of a skyscraper!' Sam J announced, his arms outstretched, like a mountaineer who'd just climbed Mount Everest.

All around them the city was densely packed with tall buildings standing upright like the bristles on a hairbrush, and where they stopped the sun was setting behind a huge expanse of silvery water dotted with all kinds of boats.

'I'm scared,' said Hannah, and sat down quickly, wrapping her arms tightly round her knees.

'Question is,' said Alice, thinking out loud, 'are we on top of the right skyscraper? Are we even in the right city? This looks like New York did. Say we are in Hong Kong, how do we know for sure this is Harbourside Tower 6?'

The two Sams were moving around the roof among a maze of pipes and boxed-in machinery. One of them found a hatch with a stiff metal fastening. Between them, they levered it off, lifted the hatch door and flopped it back onto the roof. The parrot flew over and perched on the edge of the opening. They spied a ladder inside, and called out.

'Over here!'

Alice and Edie looked at each other, and then in a single movement they both scooped Hannah up and carried her over to the hatch. She buried her head in her lap and did not even peep until she found herself inside the opening on the top step of the ladder going down. Hannah wasn't the only one with wobbly legs: they all felt a tiny bit nervous. The open hatch let a pool of light into the hallway below. Alice followed Hannah down.

As they started walking along the first corridor, blue lights set into the floor like an airport runway came on automatically. The walls were covered in silver and black stripes, and each apartment had a pair of doors that looked like a big fridge-freezer, with a wide one and a narrow one, and two long metal handles side by side in the middle. On a plaque next to each door was a number.

The boys were jumping from one blue light to the next, with the bird waddling along the carpet behind them.

'What did Charlie say the number of his Grandpa's apartment was?' Edie asked, studying each one in turn. 'We're up to 3106 here.'

'Number 3003,' Alice said.

'Well everything here starts with 31, so maybe he's on the floor below.'

They found another set of silver doors, three in a row, with a button beside each one instead of a number.

'These must be the lifts.' said Edie. 'How do we call one?'

Sam J pressed all three buttons and they stood waiting. No one was prepared to admit it, but none of them, including the parrot, had ever been in a lift before, they'd only ever seen them on TV. Above the lift doors were arrows pointing up or down. Suddenly there was a loud ping and one set of doors opened. The parrot squawked loudly and started flapping when he saw another blue parrot reflected in the mirror at the back of the lift. Alice had to pick him up and carry him inside. Sam F pressed the button that said 30, and a second later the doors opened again and they stepped out into an identical corridor. Except, as Hannah pointed out, the runway lights were pink, not blue.

The children walked past more silver and black stripes. They passed a cleaning lady in white overalls pushing a trolley along. She smiled and said something they didn't understand. And then, there they were, facing the door with 3003 written beside it.

'Aren't you going to knock, Alice?' Sam J asked in a singsong voice.

'What if he's not there?' Edie said, biting her lip. 'What if it's just his grandpa at home – we can't speak any Chinese.'

They all stood rooted to the spot. The smell of garlic was stronger than ever.

'OK, here goes.'

A maid in a white apron answered the door, and looked quite surprised to see a group of five children and a green parrot standing there. Alice asked in a clear voice, 'Is Charlie at home? We've come to see him.'

The maid smiled and welcomed them in with a sweep of her arm. She didn't say anything but she seemed to understand what Alice had said. They stepped onto thick grey carpet, and she gestured to the collection of shoes in the lobby.

'I think we're supposed to take our shoes off,' hissed Edie.

They lined up their shoes, which still had traces of St Kildan soil mixed with a yellow Amazonian variety stuck to the soles. Then they tiptoed in their socks behind the maid into the living room.

Charlie was sitting cross-legged on the floor opposite an elderly man at a glass table, and they were both eating with chopsticks out of little bowls. Charlie had his back to them and turned when he heard the maid enter the room. He nearly choked on his food when he saw his school friends standing there. He put the chopsticks down and stood up.

'Hi!' Alice said. She felt shy all of a sudden, and looked down at her socks. The Sams were giggling. Edie shot them a look of contempt and then said, 'We came to see you, Charlie.'

'I can see that, but how on earth …? Ah well, it doesn't matter, come and meet Grandpa; we were just eating our supper. Dad's not back yet. Is that … a parrot?'

'Yup,' said Edie. 'Alice found him when we went to the Amazon in the C-Bean. He wasn't supposed to come with us here. But we did leave Spex at home.'

'Spex? Who's that – a new kid in our class?'

'No. He's a dog. He came back with us accidentally from New York.' Edie said, pushing her glasses up her nose and rolling her eyes to show she knew it all sounded a bit ridiculous. The children looked embarrassed. There was a long pause.

'Cool,' said Charlie, 'now let's eat.'

Alice felt a surge of relief, and let the parrot hop off her arm and onto the sofa. Charlie moved across to the kitchen area to fetch five more bowls of garlic chicken and rice and then arranged more cushions around the table. The children sank gratefully onto their knees and picked ineptly at the rice with their chopsticks. Hannah opened up her lunchbox instead because she didn't eat chicken. Then Charlie said something in Chinese to his grandpa and the old man nodded. He wore a grey tunic and looked very wise and wrinkly.

'Lak dis,' Charlie's grandpa said, showing them how to hold the chopsticks. He chuckled with amusement as they all tried to coordinate their fingers and thumbs around the two sticks. Charlie poured out some pale looking tea that smelled of flowers from a china teapot into seven tiny cups and handed them round. Alice noticed none of the cups had handles.

'So …' he began, casually running his hand through his mop of black hair, 'Have you got something to tell me?' Charlie looked expectantly at Alice. She raised her eyebrows and pointed up at the ceiling.

'We arrived on the roof just before. You know, in the C-Bean. It was quite easy really.'

'Can I go up and see it?' he said eagerly, wiping his fingers on his checked shirt and looking much younger than almost twelve at that moment.

'Yeah. But we kind of hoped you'd show us a bit of Hong Kong while we're here.'

Charlie turned to ask his grandpa something.

'Grandpa says we can go and take a look around the harbour before it gets dark. C'mon.' Charlie picked up his mobile phone from the kitchen counter and they said goodbye to his grandpa, who bowed his head very solemnly. The maid was in the hallway arranging their shoes in a line facing the door, ready for the children to put back on.

In the lift, Charlie thumbed a text to his Dad while the Sams counted out loud from thirty down to zero, but they weren't counting quickly enough: the lift glided like silk down to the ground floor in less than ten seconds.

Alice was looking at her watch and frowning. 'Charlie, what's the time?'

'Six-fifteen.'

'Oh,' said Alice, and worked out St Kilda was eight hours behind Hong Kong. Their footsteps echoed across the marble floor of the entrance lobby as they walked towards a revolving door. Just as the children were about to go through it, the parrot got in a panic and starting flying in circles around the lobby.

The security guard was dozing at his desk, and woke up with a start when the bird squawked loudly in his ear as he flew past. The guard jumped to his feet and pressed a buzzer, but Charlie quickly ran and opened up the emergency exit at the far end of the lobby. The alarm went off but by then Alice had managed to coax the bird down. She carried him on her shoulder out of the emergency exit, leaving the alarm ringing incessantly, and several bright blue feathers whirling above the fan on the security guard's desk.

The street was teeming with people pouring in all directions from office buildings. Alice could hardly see the pavement. She looked up instead and saw wires and signs hung across the street like knitting that had come undone. Charlie was beckoning her to follow, and she could see the others were right behind him. There was a large shopping centre ahead with huge screens all over the façade showing advertisements for things in giant complicated symbols, but she couldn't understand any of them. Charlie dived down a side street that was lined on both sides with market stalls, each with its own plastic canopy and bare dangling light bulb. Alice wanted to look at all the things they were selling, but she didn't want to lose the others like she had the last time. A little way ahead, Charlie stopped.

When she caught up they were standing in front of a stall that seemed to be selling all kinds of shrivelled up dead animals, some in jars, others in transparent plastic boxes. Dead snakes, rhinoceros horns, beetles, spiders, birds, and many other creatures and parts of creatures Alice couldn't identify.

'What do people buy this stuff for? Souvenirs?'

'They make medicines out of it. Chinese people believe it will make them live longer. Some things they eat as a delicacy – like those bird's nests.' Charlie was pointing at some yellowy-brown saucer-shaped things wrapped in cellophane.

'Bird's nests?' Sam J wanted to check he had heard right.

'Yeah, these ones cost five thousand Hong Kong dollars a box.'

'No way!'

Alice stood fingering one of the smaller boxes containing an almost transparent seahorse. She noticed that Edie was standing well back, holding tight onto Hannah's hand. The air was close, and people were pushing past with bags of groceries. They walked to the end of the night market and turned into a quieter, darker road. The Sams were whispering about something.

There was a very strange smell. On the corner there was a fruit seller sitting on an upturned crate. She had arranged all kinds of fruit on a sheet of grubby cardboard in front of her. One of the fruits was as big as a football and covered in brown spikes.

'Charlie, what's that?' Alice asked.

'Ah, they're durians. It's called the King of Fruits here. That's what the smell is; Dad says it's like sick mixed with dead rats and smelly socks!'

'Do people really eat it?'

'Yeah. I've tried it. It's a bit like onion-flavoured custard. But it smells so bad on the outside, you're not allowed to take it in the subway trains or in any of the shopping centres.'

Alice reached down and touched the fruit. It was like an enormous seabean. The fruitseller picked it up and handed it to her. She cradled it in her arms, thinking how it weighed about the same as her baby brother. But it felt rough and cool like a rock.

'Charlie have you got any money? I really want to buy this thing.'

'What for?'

'To put on the nature table at school.'

'You're mad, Alice.' Charlie laughed and fished in his pocket for some money to haggle with the fruit seller. A minute later Alice was walking happily along, swinging the heavy fruit in a plastic bag.

'C'mon, this way,' Charlie shepherded them all across the road. The parrot squawked as if to reinforce his instruction and transferred himself to Charlie's shoulder, sensing he was now the leader. Through a brightly lit doorway they saw a group of men in green overalls crowded round a television cheering loudly at a horse race on the screen. When it was over, they handed each other money. The six children crossed the road in the darkness and realised there were no more buildings here, just a wide pavement. Alice could hear the sloshing of water against a wall. The sound was suddenly so familiar, she closed her eyes and was right back in Village Bay down by the seawall, listening to the waves lapping against the pier. She breathed in, hoping to smell the strong clean St Kilda air, but this air was full of diesel, rotting fruit and fish.

All along the harbour, fishing boats had drawn up, and fishermen were busy hauling their catch in crates onto the dockside. The two Sams ran on ahead to look in the boxes. There were men hosing down the decks as the boats bobbed and knocked against the harbour wall.

'Look at the size of these fish!' Sam J was riveted. 'That one's got like a sword coming off the end of its nose.'

'And some are still alive!' shrieked Sam F.

'We've got enough pets now,' said Edie firmly, but they all stood and looked at the writhing mass of silvery fish in the nearest crate. All except Charlie, who was sending another text.

There was one boat that did not look the same as the others, or at least it was not unloading fish. There was a crate on the dockside with some tall metal cylinders in it that looked like silver fire extinguishers. The boat was bright green, and on the side Alice could see a logo with a name. There was something familiar about it. She went a little closer and saw the name was written in a logo she recognised: Eldorado Brasil.

Alice stopped swinging the shopping bag, and her stomach lurched as she remembered the caterpillar truck. She could see someone inside the boat's cabin looking at some maps. On the deck were eight or nine other crates containing rows of the same dull metal cylinders. The man in the cabin came out, and when he looked up she felt sure she recognised the same dark face and yellow baseball cap she'd seen before in the rainforest. He glared at her, or rather at the parrot, who flinched on her shoulder, his claws gripping her collarbone tightly. Alice could sense that the man and the bird knew each other.

Just as Charlie said, 'It's dark, we need to get back to the apartment,' a surly-looking gang appeared, and Alice saw they were the same men they'd just seen gambling on the horse race. A short fat man lunged for the parrot, but Charlie caught his arm as Alice ducked and ran towards the fishermen. She called to the boys 'Sam! Sam! Run!'

The boys obeyed instantly, but she couldn't see any sign of Edie or Hannah.

The parrot flew from Alice's shoulder onto the deck of one of the fishing boats, and squawked excitedly. He kept saying '*vamos, vamos*' to the men. The fishermen, thinking he was after their catch, began shouting at the him, and slid their boxes across the wet dockside out of reach. The man in the yellow cap jumped ashore and was now coming towards them. Alice waited behind some crates until he got close and then swung for him with the durian. She caught him by surprise. The man slipped, and unable to regain his balance, fell backwards into the water. The other men didn't stop to rescue him, but came after Alice and Charlie, who were by now heading back towards the night market, calling for the parrot to follow.

Charlie had taken one of the metal cylinders from the crate and, holding it like a baseball bat, swung it at two of the men. He missed and held the cylinder out in front of him to keep the others at bay, all the while running backwards along the dockside. Finally he turned and ran, the cylinder tucked under his arm.

Alice stumbled after him, past the fruit seller and up the busy street that was now crowded with tourists. She pushed past them, craning her neck upwards looking for the parrot, willing him to follow her. She could hear police sirens, and emerged at the crossing opposite Charlie's apartment building. She could see the security guard standing by the plate glass window, watching as the commotion built up in the street outside. She turned back and saw Charlie, Hannah and Edie a few metres away. But there was no sign of either Sam.

'Alice! This way!' She looked back across the street. The boys had opened the emergency exit and beckoned to her. When the lights changed, she slipped through the crowd, crossed the road and stood on the pavement, calling for the startled bird. At last she caught sight of some blue feathers, and he swooped in through the door just ahead of her. The security guard was at the other end of the lobby facing away from them, and there might just be enough time to run across to the lifts before he had time to react.

She pummelled the buttons outside the lifts, summoning them under her breath. The one on the right arrived first, and Alice and the two Sams got in to shrieks of 'perigroso, perigroso' like a demented old lady. There wasn't time to wait for the others, because the security guard was already heading their way. The doors slid shut and they began their ascent to the thirtieth floor.

Alice banged on the door to Charlie's grandpa's apartment but there was no reply. An alarm started ringing again in the corridor, and when Charlie, Edie and Hannah stepped out of the next lift, Alice said hurriedly 'Let's go up to the C-Bean and wait there until it's all quietened down.'

Charlie nodded, and led the way up the final flight of stairs and onto the roof, still carrying the metal cylinder. The C-Bean loomed mysteriously in the moonlight, surrounded by the billowing clouds of steam from the air conditioning units. Alice said 'hello' as she approached the door, and stepped back to let Charlie go in first. She stood and waited for all the children to come out of the hatch. But there was no sign of the parrot.

She looked up into the night sky, willing him to return, and suddenly he exploded out of the hatch and started to wheel around above the building. He flew higher and higher, his squawks getting fainter as he got further away, until Alice thought she would never see him again. She was about to close the door of the C-Bean, when a vision of blue flashed through the cloud of steam. The bird landed rather ungracefully and then waddled across to the door, muttering to himself and shaking his head from side to side. Alice ushered him into the C-Bean and closed the door gently behind him.

Charlie was talking to someone on his mobile phone. The other kids looked exhausted and sat on the floor. Alice's mind was still racing through the streets down below. She put down the durian finally.

'That thing really does smell, Alice, why'd you have to get it?' asked Edie.

'She did knock the man that was after us into the water with it,' pointed out Sam J.

'Yeah, that was way cool, Alice,' murmured Sam F.

'Did any of you recognise him? The bird did – I mean from the rainforest – I think he was after the parrot, not me,' said Alice.

Charlie finished his phone call. 'Sorry, that was my Dad. He says I'm grounded. I can't believe it, you guys show up, I ask if I can show you round, and it's only just gone dark, but Dad gets crazy with me, says there's all kinds of bad people who hang out down by the harbour.'

'Well, we did run in to a few,' Alice observed.

'I suppose so – who were those guys, do you think?'

'Pirates!' said Sam J.

'Yeah, right,' said Edie dismissively.

'What's in the cylinder, Charlie? Maybe that will give us a clue,' Alice suggested.

Charlie looked at his impromptu weapon for the first time. The label was in Chinese but written in characters he couldn't read. There was, however, a warning symbol they could all recognise: a skull and crossbones.

'See, told you it was pirates!' Sam looked triumphant.

'Der! That just means that whatever is inside it is dangerous,' said Edie sarcastically.

'*Perigroso, perigroso*' chirped the parrot nervously.

'Is that what it means when he says that – danger?' Alice wondered.

The C-Bean, which had been completely unresponsive until then, flickered into life, and across the four walls started to display hundreds of words written in black in all different languages and writing systems. The words pulsed round the walls for a few seconds, and then stopped, and certain words turned red.

The children stood up to inspect the red words. Both 'danger' and 'perigroso' appeared. When they touched the words, the C-Bean said them out loud.

'Wow,' said Charlie, 'this thing is amazing! How does it do all this stuff?' Among all the other words, he recognised the Chinese character for danger: *wei*. It looked like a person curled up in a ball hiding under a roof.

Alice had an idea.

'Charlie, put the cylinder on the table, so the label is facing down.' Charlie held the cylinder on its side so it wouldn't roll off, and the table, which had been blank until now, began to process information. A strange diagram like a hundred square began to appear, only each coloured square had letters written in it as well as numbers. The diagram was not a complete shape, but was jagged along the top. It looked a bit like a city skyline. One of the squares down near the bottom right began to flash. It had the letters 'Hg' written inside it. Alice touched the square and beside the diagram a single word appeared: mercury. Then a map appeared next to it, showing where mercury came from. There were places marked in grey where mercury ore was no longer mined, and only one place was coloured red, to indicate mercury was still being mined: China.

'That's it. It's mercury. Dad told me about it. It's a poisonous metal they use to extract gold. Someone must be smuggling it from Hong Kong to the gold miners in Brazil, Charlie!' Alice's eyes shone with fear and excitement.

'What on earth are you talking about, Alice?'

'The boat in the harbour had the same logo on it as the one I saw on a truck in the rainforest: Eldorado Brasil. They must be connected.'

'Shhhh,' said Edie, 'Can you hear something outside?'

They all listened. They could hear footsteps and then there was a loud knock on the side of the C-Bean.

'We better get going,' said Edie.

'What about Charlie? He can't come back to St Kilda with us.'

'I'll text my Dad and say I'm staying over at a friend's.'

'But you're grounded.'

'Well I'm not going outside now, am I? We don't know who's out there. C'mon, how do you work this thing?'

While Charlie texted his father, Alice took a deep breath and said 'TO ST KILDA'. The children waited in silence. They could hear footsteps walking round the perimeter of the C-Bean, and people using walkie-talkies. In another moment they were gone.

A lice knew something had gone wrong because they couldn't seem to open the door to get out of the C-Bean. Nor had the walls become porous for them to step through like before. But they had arrived somewhere. Outside they could hear music and a crowd of voices, and a series of loud bangs that sounded like gunshots. Except every time the bangs stopped, they could hear voices cheering.

Suddenly there was a knock on the door, and someone shouted, 'Hurry up in there, I need to pee!' They had a strong accent, but it was not Scottish, Chinese or American.

Charlie said, 'Now what do we do?'

Alice was rummaging around in her schoolbag for the instruction manual. She opened the digital book and thumbed anxiously through the index. There were entries for problem diagnosis, system malfunction and manual or remote override. The problem section listed all kinds of issues, including '*C-Bean non-responsive*' and '*involuntary system shut-down*'. Both entries suggested that the C-Bean could be malfunctioning due to electrical storms, magnetic interference, or excess heat or cold. Its operating range was given as being between 50 degrees centigrade and minus 50 degrees centigrade. It had been hot in Hong Kong, but Alice felt sure it was nowhere near the maximum.

'Charlie, was there any telecommunications equipment on the roof of your apartment building?' she asked.

'Could be. The whole building has wireless 5G super-broadband access.'

Then Alice remembered Charlie had been using his phone as they departed.

'Something has messed up the transport function. We're going to have to reset the C-Bean.'

'How do you do that?'

'I don't know – we'll just have to follow the instructions in here.'

Sam J was munching a sandwich from his lunchbox, and Hannah was drawing pictures of the strange fruit and shrivelled up animals she'd seen in her sketchbook.

'How long will that take? Cos I need a pee too,' Sam J announced.

Alice scanned through the section titled 'How to reset your C-Bean Mark 3'. First, it said, evacuate the cabin.

Fine, we can't do that, thought Alice. Then, using the external keypad, re-key the serial number which is embossed on the card key, followed by three Xs. Then hold down the green button for ten seconds.

'How on earth do we do that when we can't even get out?' wondered Alice aloud.

'Do what?' Charlie asked impatiently. 'Let me see!'

'The reset routine only works if you are outside the C-Bean. We're stuck inside.'

'Isn't there some kind of code word we can use, or something?' Edie suggested.

'Genius, Edie!' said Alice.

Alice tried to think. When she said Hello, the C-Bean opened the door to let her in. So what if she simply said Goodbye?

They heard a mechanism unlatch, and the person outside flung open the door and burst in with a bemused look on his face.

'Who are you?' Sam F was staring at the boy and blocking the doorway like a proficient nightclub bouncer. 'This is not a toilet, OK?'

'OK, I thought this was the loo block, mate,' the boy said, rolling his eyes. 'That's the trouble with festivals – there are never enough places to pee.'

'Festival? What festival?' Sam continued his interrogation with a rising note of panic in his voice.

'St Kilda Festival, you dimwit. What's this, some kind of meeting of the Melbourne Secret Society?'

Sam F pushed past the boy, and stepped out onto a sandy patch of dried up grass in front of an esplanade of palm trees. It was pitch black and very hot, and coming up the middle of the colonnade was a loud marching band. The man at the front was wearing a leopard skin tunic and beating a drum. High above his head, and merging with the night sky, waved a large dark blue flag covered in stars with a tiny Union Jack in the corner.

Charlie stood beside Alice, blinking in disbelief. The others came out of the C-Bean like frightened rabbits and stood with their hands over their ears as the procession filed past.

'Welcome to Australia, aliens!' the boy said, and walked off.

Suddenly the night sky exploded into colour. Fireworks lit up crowds of faces picnicking under the palm trees, and illuminated the suburban houses that ran along the edge of the esplanade. In the other direction, the children could see in the brief intense flashes of light a pier stretching out into the sea, and a long sandy beach.

Alice recognised the scene from her jigsaw puzzle and grinned.

'Awesome! This is the other St Kilda. Remember – the one Reverend Sinclair told us about once? Where the people from our St Kilda arrived by boat over a hundred and fifty years ago.'

'But why have we arrived here?' Charlie looked perplexed.

'I dunno. The C-Bean must have been thrown off course – it understood the instruction for St Kilda, but because of the interference from your mobile, it came here instead of Scotland.'

'Cool,' said Charlie, watching a huge white firework die away to blues and reds.

They could smell some delicious food cooking, and realised that the C-Bean had landed next to a cluster of brick-built barbecues, where people were grilling fresh fish.

'I'm hungry,' Sam J said, salivating in front of the nearest barbecue.

'We haven't got any money,' pointed out Edie.

'I have,' said Hannah, and fished some coins out of her jeans pocket.

'It's Scottish money. You need Australian money here.'

'We can try. I've got some Hong Kong dollars too, remember – c'mon,' said Charlie.

The men running the barbecue were starting to pack up, and said the children would get something to eat for free if they mucked in. Sam F and Sam J looked ecstatic: they were both given striped aprons to wear, and a knife each to slit open pitta bread to make grilled fish sandwiches.

'Where are you kids from exactly? Sydney?'

'No, we're from the real St Kilda,' said Edie solemnly.

'Whad'ya mean the real one – this is the real McCoy here!'

'We're from an island called St Kilda off the west coast of Scotland.'

'I thought no one lived there any more,' said one of the chefs.

'They didn't until five years ago. We went out to live there because our parents are setting up a wave energy plant,' explained Alice.

'Oh, now I get why you guys are here. This is now the main environmental festival of the year, ain't that right, Geoff? All kinds of alternative energy people are here as well as all the music and stuff. Including the wave guys – there are a several wave energy companies operating in Australia too. Beats using charcoal. That's best left for barbies, eh Geoff! You like tomato salsa on your fish, kids?'

They handed the children a portion of food each, a couple of bottles of homemade lemonade, and a leaflet about the festival.

'Tonight's the last night – crikey it's already ten-thirty – only another few hours to go 'til next year,' Geoff remarked.

The six children thanked the two men, and wandered over to the seaside promenade to sit on a bench and eat their food. Alice recalled it was only seven-thirty when they left Hong Kong, so they were a few hours ahead again. Another place, another time zone. It was all a bit dizzying. She stared out to sea, and instead of trying to place herself somewhere in time, she tried to picture where she was on her illuminated globe.

'That's Antarctica out there,' she said after a minute or two.

'How do you know?' Sam J said with his mouth full.

'Well, Melbourne is at the bottom of Australia, and there's nothing below it except miles of sea, and then tons of icebergs, and then the South Pole.'

'Hey, there's penguins!' said Sam J.

'Don't be stupid, there aren't any penguins in Australia,' Edie protested.

'Look, here!' Sam pointed at an advert in the leaflet, showing a picture of some little penguins waddling along the beach near St Kilda, looking like a family going home after a day at the seaside.

The children all laughed and both Sams started doing imitations of penguins waddling.

'Where's our parrot?' said Alice suddenly. 'I don't remember him getting out of the C-Bean.'

They finished their food and threw the napkins into a bin on the seafront, then walked back to the C-Bean. There inside was the bird, cowering under his wing and refusing to move.

'I think he's a bit traumatised,' said Alice, concerned.

'What should we do?' Edie asked. 'I vote we go back now. We've got to work out how to get the C-Bean to work again properly, right?'

Alice picked him up and gently wrapped him in her cardigan. She emptied her bag and put the parrot inside with just his head poking out, saying 'There, there,' like she'd heard her mum say to Kit when he was crying.

'Nah,' said Charlie, still poring over the leaflet. 'I vote we take a look round the festival just until it's over. There's all sorts happening.'

As Charlie was the oldest, the decision went his way. Edie was already fretting and saying they had to all stick together.

As they moved towards the main street, they could hear someone making a speech through a loudhailer. A crowd had gathered round a small platform, waving banners and placards saying 'Stop Poisoning our Rivers!' and 'Whales and Dolphins Deserve Better!' Alice persuaded the others to stand and listen.

A man in a flowery shirt took the loudhailer from the person standing next to him. He had rolled his sleeves up and Alice could see sweat pouring down his neck. He loosened his tie and cleared his throat.

'You want to know something?' he began. 'In the past year two whales and three dolphins had been found beached on the Melbourne coastline. The Yarra River is still as polluted as ever, with heavy metals present in the water long after the gold mines had closed upstream. In my opinion, and it's one supported by a number of leading experts I can tell you, mercury and other substances are getting into the food chain and severely affecting the well-being of our marine mammals, making them confused and disorientated.'

Alice was trying hard to follow, but the man's voice was becoming quite emotional: 'That's why,' he went on, 'they are getting beached. It is wrong, and something needs to be done!' He lowered the loudhailer from his mouth and stepped down from the platform. The crowd applauded and cheered. Alice thought he sounded just like her dad when you got him started on something he cared about.

Charlie was moving off. The bird was fidgeting inside her bag, so Alice lifted him out and onto her shoulder. They walked on up the street, where there were stalls giving away free T-shirts and mugs as well as leaflets about a whole variety of environmental causes. Sam J spotted a stall about the Phillip Island penguin colony.

'Hey look Alice, they're called Fairy Penguins. It says there are hundreds of them near here!'

Alice was thinking about the hundred dead seabirds she'd counted at Gleann Mor. She wanted to ask someone about it. Just then someone tapped her on the shoulder. She turned round and a very tall woman with piercing blue eyes was looking not at her, but at the parrot.

'What are you doing with a rare endangered species?' she demanded suspiciously.

Alice shrugged. 'We found him. He was injured.'

'Found him? Where?'

Alice didn't know what to say. Who was this woman, and why did she want to know? Charlie stepped in, 'It's none of your business, my Dad got him from an animal rescue place in Hong Kong.'

'Let me take a look at him. I'm a vet. I have a stall over this way. I work for an Animal Protection Agency. Come with me,' she commanded. The children looked at each other. They were tired of running away, so they followed meekly after her.

The woman took the bird and placed him on the table behind her stall. 'If I'm not mistaken, this is a Spix's Macaw – it's native to Brazil and as far as I know is now virtually extinct in the wild, did you know that?' she said accusingly, as she spread out his wing and tail feathers.

'No, we didn't know,' Alice said, wondering if the vet was going to confiscate their parrot.

'Hey, cool, Alice,' said Sam J. 'We can call him Spix!'

'Yeah, then we've got a Spix and a Spex,' added Sam F.

Spix clucked approvingly at his new name. Although he appeared a bit affronted at the vet's examination, he sensed he was in expert hands.

'He says things,' said Sam J.

'Ah yes, they're very good mimics,' the woman said, sounding a little more relaxed.

'He says stuff like "perigroso",' Sam went on amiably.

'Hmm, Hong Kong you said. Why does he say things in Portuguese, I wonder?' said the vet.

'Is he going to be OK? His tail, I mean?' Alice asked, changing the subject.

'Yes, there are no broken bones. But he should be living in a rainforest, not being kept as a child's pet.' She gave Spix a seed from her pocket and watched him shell and eat it. 'No problems with his eating and drinking?'

'No, I don't think so.'

'They eat the fruit of the swamp almond tree where they come from, but a lot of the forests where the tree grows are being devastated. So the bird's natural habitat is slowly being destroyed. Here – read this.'

The vet handed them another leaflet with a picture of a parrot very like Spix on the front cover. Spix hopped back onto Alice's shoulder, and bobbing his head, said over and over, '*Muito mau. Vamos, vamos.*'

'What's he saying?' asked Sam F.

'If I'm not mistaken, he's saying something like, Very bad, very bad, go away,' laughed the vet.

The children wandered back towards the seafront. They had been swept down a different street by the crowds leaving the festival, who were now congregating at the tram stops and bus stops, waiting to go home. They could see a huge sign marked 'Luna Park' up ahead, and could hear screams and fairground music spilling out. The children stared longingly through the ticket barriers at the whirling and cavorting rides inside. Then they walked around the perimeter of the amusement park, where some little striped tents had been erected. There were signs propped up outside each one, offering fortune-telling, crystal ball gazing and palmistry.

An old lady with curly white hair stepped out of one of the tents, and smiled at the children. Alice looked at her apprehensively, and the woman beckoned to her. There was something familiar about her.

'Come child, I can tell you are troubled. Let me show you something.'

Charlie said to Alice, 'Have you ever had your palm read or been told what will happen to you in the future?'

'Can they really do that?'

'They say they can. Lots of people say it's all guesswork.'

'Shall I go, Charlie?'

'Yeah, why not? We'll wait for you right outside. I'll make sure nothing happens.'

Alice followed the woman into her tent, and sat down on the little stool. The old lady sat opposite, behind a table covered in a cloth marked with what looked like a noughts and crosses grid.

'I practise Kumalak, my dear Alice. It's a system of fortune-telling from Kazakhstan that's been used for more than a thousand years.'

'How do you know my name?'

'What is your question?'

'I don't know what you mean?'

'The one thing you want to know, tell me, what is it?'

Alice thought hard while the woman chanted mechanically under her breath. She felt she wanted to ask a lot of questions. But what did she want to know exactly? She felt as if the sea was surging through her, oily black waves crashing through her chest. She felt dangerous chemicals tingling in her fingertips and on the tip of her tongue, and the sharp dryness in her throat she had felt in the rainforest. There were monkeys, parrots, chainsaws and her baby brother creating a cacophony in her tired brain.

She took a deep breath, and felt the old woman in front of her disappear and instead the female warrior was there again, confronting her from long ago, her warm hands touching her hair.

'I want to know why.'

The old woman nodded and pulled out a little bag. She emptied out a pile of beans from the bag and divided them into three piles. Alice counted forty-one beans in total. The old lady began by touching each one to her forehead, dividing them up among the nine squares in front of her, according to some ancient formula. She looked up at Alice from time to time, as if she was trying to work out what she was thinking. At last the beans were all distributed to her satisfaction, and the woman spread her hands out on the table.

'There. Now let's see,' she began. 'The number three is about the three realms of nature: animal, vegetable and mineral. For you, these have become powerfully interconnected. Your question of why seeks to learn the links between them and how these become broken, in nature as well as in your own life.'

Alice tried to concentrate on what the old lady was saying. She felt so tired, and the sound of seagulls outside was making her homesick. The woman continued.

'Three beans in this square tells me you are caught up in a vivid journey, full of strange encounters, and that from this you are gathering new strength. You are far from home, and even there you have encountered changes, dangers and unsettling news. You must return, and apply what you have learned.'

Alice felt a little overwhelmed. It was as if the woman had looked at her under a microscope and seen all the fuzzy teeming particles as an overall pattern. But it still didn't make sense. She just knew that she was on the other side of the world and she needed to get back home. The woman smiled knowingly to herself, and scooped the beans back into the bag.

Alice looked in her pockets for something to give her by way of payment. At first all she could find were a few seeds the vet had given her. Then she found the two-pound coin Dad gave her on her birthday for the cream cake. She laid the coin on the table, thanked her and left.

'So are you going to marry me and live happily ever after, then?' Charlie teased when she came out. He grinned but Alice looked stern and serious.

'Nothing like that, no. C'mon, we need to get back to the C-Bean,' she said, and strode at great speed down the street towards the esplanade.

Alice took great care inputting the correct St Kilda coordinates this time, and made Charlie switch off his mobile phone. The jolt came sooner and more fiercely than usual. Even after the C-Bean had apparently arrived at its destination, it seemed to rock unsteadily on its base. Alice could hear wind gusting and waves pounding right outside. There was a sudden crack of thunder and the C-Bean shuddered.

'Great. I've arrived back home in the middle of the worst thunderstorm ever,' said Charlie, rolling his eyes.

'At least we made it,' remarked Alice.

'I sincerely hope so,' said Edie.

Silence.

Another thunderclap tore open the door suddenly. To begin with all they could see was a mass of angry clouds and rain sheeting down onto a choppy grey sea. It was impossible to tell if it was night or day. In the midst of a flash of lightning Alice could see it was their St Kilda, sure enough: across the bay she could see the familiar misty outline of the smaller island of Dun. In the same moment she realised, however, they had not arrived in the schoolyard, but were instead perched precariously on the jagged landing rocks along the coast, just above the gun emplacement.

As they all moved towards the door to peer out, the C-Bean tipped abruptly towards the sea, and the children clung onto each other in terror. Over the roar of the waves, Alice barked at the others to go back to the far side of the cabin and stay there. As a result, the C-Bean shifted in the opposite direction and seemed to wedge itself into the rocks. Charlie crawled on his hands and knees back to where Alice stood gripping the edge of the door, and they both looked out and assessed the situation. Edie let go of Spix, who was struggling to get free and join Charlie, but he was blown out of the door before he could manage to land on Charlie's shoulder.

Alice leaned out, calling 'Spix! Come back!' An enormous wave crashed on the rocks below and threw up a huge spume of spray. The last thing she remembered was that she couldn't see the parrot. Then a sudden gust of wind must have slammed the door shut and caught Alice sharply on the head and knocked her out cold.

The old lady was throwing hundreds of seabeans up into the air, crying 'Kumalak, kumalak'. Alice was running around trying to pick them all up again and put them back in the little bag. Every time she picked one up, it turned into a dead fish, or a dead bird, and the seabean was its beady silver eye staring up at her. The silver eyes became blobs of silver liquid that trickled out, and Alice tried to pick it up, but it was impossible. It spilled through her fingers in tiny silver balls and ran in all directions...

When she came to, Alice's head was throbbing violently. Edie and Charlie had done their best to clean the wound on her scalp with salt water and had wound a sweater around it.

'Are you feeling OK, Alice?' Edie asked. Alice was lying in her lap and it was pitch black inside the C-Bean.

'A bit sick,' she admitted. 'How long have I been unconscious?'

'About half an hour,' said Charlie from a dark corner. Alice could hear the other children breathing.

'I think the C-Bean is pretty badly damaged, Alice,' said Edie, breaking the news to her friend as gently as she could.

But Alice was only dimly aware of where she was. 'It smells in here, have I been sick?' she asked.

'No, it's that spiky fruit you got, remember!' said Sam J, and he rummaged around in the dark to find the malodorous durian and pulled it out of its plastic bag.

Alice was feeling distinctly nauseous now, and retched loudly. Charlie crawled across the floor to open the door. The wind had dropped, but the sudden movement caused the C-Bean to lurch again and shift position. The durian rolled rapidly across the floor, making a strange ticking sound as its spikes grazed the floor, and fell into the sea below. Charlie watched as it resurfaced, and laughed.

'Well, that's two passengers down. Only six more to go. Who's next?'

'I don't know what you think is so funny – your Dad'll be worried sick about where you are,' said Edie reproachfully.

'Let's not talk about being sick, shall we. The smell is bad enough in here as it is,' retorted Charlie. 'Alice, are you up to a bit of rock-climbing?'

Alice groaned softly, and said, 'No way'.

Charlie had an idea. 'Edie, what's your Mum's phone number?'

He switched his phone back on, thumbed the number, including the Scottish dialling code, and waited for someone in the Burney house to answer. There was no reply.

'Any other numbers I should try?'

Alice said weakly, 'Call my Mum, Charlie, she'll be at home with Kit.'

Charlie tried again. 'Mrs Robertson? Is that you? It's Charlie.' The line was very crackly and he could hardly hear what Alice's mum was saying, and then the line cut out.

'How long have we been away roughly?' Edie asked.

Alice managed to lift her arm and look at the glowing hands on her watch. 'Five hours or so.'

'Perhaps we should try and call the air rescue people,' said Edie. 'They'd be able to get us off the rock safely.'

'Air rescue,' repeated Alice drowsily, and passed out.

She could hear helicopter blades scuttering round above their heads. Next she was dangling from a long rope with someone's arms wrapped round her. Seawater in her eyes and nose. Then there was a blanket that smelled of something strange. Dad's face with anxious eyes. Someone stroking her hair.

Alice missed the worst of the trouble their trip to Hong Kong had caused. It was two days after they'd arrived back on the island before she regained consciousness properly. The worst was definitely when the grown-ups realised Charlie Cheung was among the children that had been rescued, but there was no sign of his Dad. Charlie was more concerned there was no sign of a parrot, and that's when Edie's mum, who was treating all the children for shock and hypothermia, decided that Charlie must have hit his head too.

A few days later Charlie brought round the newspapers for Alice to read. Several newspapers had sent reporters over from the mainland to cover the story of the island children who had been blown onto the cliffs in their mobile classroom/stranded on the mountain in a storm/abducted by aliens, depending on which paper you read. They mostly reported that by the time the Scottish authorities had contacted Charlie's Dad in Hong Kong, he'd already filed Charlie as a missing person when he didn't return home that evening.

One of the reports also noted, but made clear the events were not necessarily linked, that bizarrely the police had also carried out a raid in the vicinity of the Cheung's apartment building. There had been reports, it said, about a cache of illegal mercury found at the harbour as well as sightings of a UFO on the roof of Harbourside Tower 6. Neither the alleged mercury nor the UFO had been found.

'So how long have you been grounded for this time, Charlie?' Alice asked as she handed back the newspapers.

'Forever, I should imagine. Dad thinks I took my air ticket from the apartment and flew back to Scotland by myself, and was brought over from the mainland in the air rescue helicopter. As far as he's concerned it's the only logical explanation, so that's what I've let him believe. But the good thing is, I've been grounded here. Dad flew back yesterday, and we're staying put now.'

'That's great.'

They fell silent. Alice sat up in bed and felt the bandage covering her left eye and most of her head. She could hear Spex barking outside.

'What do you think of Spex?'

'That's another story. When you lot disappeared, apparently he did too, so they all thought that wherever you were, Spex was with you. Then it turned out he'd been staying with Old Jim in his hovel up the hill. The next morning, Mr McLintock saw Spex pestering some grey seals down on the beach.'

'I like that he found Jim. One lonely waif and stray meets another.'

Alice's Dad came in carrying a tray of scrambled eggs and toast.

'Hi Charlie, feeling better? Here's your lunch, Alice. Eat up. Then, if you're feeling up to it, we can have a gentle stroll down to the Evaw shed this afternoon, because today is Launch Day!'

'You're launching the wave energy machines already?' Charlie was incredulous.

'Yes, your Dad said the last tests he ran in Hong Kong on the control system worked a treat, so we're going for it – two months ahead of schedule!' Alice's Dad rubbed his hands together with excitement. Then suddenly he looked all gloomy and forlorn.

'It's just a shame about the hundred thousand pounds we still need to buy the island – that's going to be an impossibly difficult task to achieve, I'd say, considering we've only got about ten weeks to go before the deadline. Shame. Those wretched Russians and their oil rigs. Everyone was looking forward to having a massive party to celebrate stopping all that!'

Alice's Dad got up and left the room.

'We've got to do something, Charlie, it's not right.'

'Yeah, but time's not exactly on our side, is it?'

'Anyway, what about the C-Bean's control system?' Alice asked, changing the subject.

'Ah. Sorry, more bad news. There was no sign of the instruction manual when they searched inside. Or the mercury cylinder. And there are no plans to get the C-Bean off the rocks for now. They are saying it's too difficult and they're going to leave it there 'til the weather is better, and then try to winch it off the rocks. But it'll be expensive. I suppose there's a chance we could get it working again.'

Alice looked bitterly disappointed and pulled the covers over her head. Charlie waited a few minutes for the sobbing to stop, and then slipped out of her room. In the end, both Alice and Kit slept through the Evaw launch, but their mother watched from the kitchen window as the last of the huge pieces of machinery and long orange floats were manoeuvred out into the sombre grey sea.

Alice's next visitor was waiting patiently by her bedside when she woke the next morning. The first thing she saw when she opened her eyes were fluorescent yellow shoelaces.

'Dr Foster!'

'Alice, it's so good to see you again. Gee, what a lot of things have happened while I've been gone!' Alice thought he reminded her of someone else, but she couldn't think who it was.

'I'm so sorry about the C-Bean. We shouldn't have gone in it without you there. I'm sorry we've got it stuck on the rocks.'

'Now don't fret about all that, Alice. Normal school is starting again on Monday, so I thought I would bring you over some books to read, if you are feeling up to it.' Dr Foster sounded more business-like now.

Alice nodded. She was staring at her illuminated globe and wondering if they'd ever go on any more adventures in the C-Bean. She closed her eyes and drifted off to sleep.

She dreamed she was in the C-Bean, but inside it was as if she was floating in a warm pool with her baby brother in her arms. She was kissing him and feeding him sunflower seeds and he was making appreciative little gurgling noises. When she looked down he seemed to have a little fishy tail like a mermaid. The tail was swishing backwards and forwards in the water, so Alice let go to see if he could swim. He paddled towards the table in the centre, which was like a little island in the middle of the pool of water, and grabbed onto the edge.

'Good boy,' she cooed, 'good boy!'

Spex licked her face, pleased to see Alice awake again, and judging by how fast his tail wagged, he obviously thought she was talking to him.

The first day Alice felt well enough to go back to school, the sun was shining. She saw primroses flowering in the grass and puffins returning to nest in their burrows on the cliffs. When she arrived at school, the classroom smelled a bit strange, like someone had left some very sweaty socks on the radiator overnight. Dr Foster had placed a large bag on his desk.

'Now come over here, kids, I've got something exciting to show you.'

The six children came forward to stand in front of Dr Foster's desk, feeling a little uneasy.

'Remember on my very first day I showed you a seabean, and I told you that sometimes you can find things washed up on the beach from far far away? This morning I went for my morning stroll along the bay, and caught sight of a large round object on the beach. At first I thought it was a coco de mer, which is a kind of seabean that can float many hundreds of miles, but now I think it's something quite different. See what you think. It's got a very strange smell.'

He unzipped the bag and pulled out Alice's durian. On one side the spiky brown skin was broken and they could see the inside of the fruit. Some of the spikes had been snapped off by the storm waves, and it no longer looked as fresh as when they'd bought it. Alice and Charlie exchanged glances, and then Charlie put up his hand.

'Yes, Charlie?'

'You can get those in Hong Kong. It's called a …'

'… King of Fruits,' the children all chimed together, and laughed.

Dr Foster looked very surprised and pleased at the evident enthusiasm of his students.

'Very good! Now, Charlie, can you make up a card for it, and as it's King of the Fruits, you can put it over there in pride of place on the nature table.'

Dr Foster pointed to the nature table, and noticed that something else was already occupying pride of place. He walked across to the table, and the children started fidgeting nervously. Sam J pulled his face and pretended to bite his finger.

'Now, what's this? I see something's been added to our little collection while I've been away.' In between the mermaid's purse and the hamburger seedpod sat the gold nugget. The teacher picked it up and turned it slowly in his hands.

'Now that's heavy. Where did you find it?'

Silence.

'Come on; let me in on the secret. Whatever is it?'

More silence.

'Well, I have an idea of what it is, but it seems quite improbable …'

Sam J could hardly contain himself.

'It's a lump of gold and we found it when …'

Edie butted in, 'Well, it looks like gold, but actually it's a rock that we found near Gleann Mor and we painted to make it look like a lump of real gold.'

'Is that so? Well, it's very realistic – and very heavy. If it was real, it would be worth a lot of money.'

Sam F raised his eyebrows. 'How much would it be worth, Dr Foster?'

'Let's weigh it, shall we, and work it out.'

The lump turned out to weigh 2.5 kilogrammes. Dr Foster said that gold was worth about sixty thousand dollars a kilo.

Edie was the quickest. 'Dr Foster, that's a hundred-and-fifty thousand dollars' worth of gold. I mean if it was real, that is.'

'Very good, pity it isn't, that's what I say.'

Alice felt faint and went into the toilets to fetch herself a glass of water. She stared out of the window at the green slopes of Conachair stretching into the distance. How much did Dad say they still needed to buy their island? A hundred thousand …

Her train of thought was broken by a noise outside the window.

'*Perigroso, muito mau, muito mau.*'

'Spix!'

Alice was overjoyed to see the missing parrot hopping along the stone wall outside. He looked up at her and ruffled his feathers against the wind.

Alice opened the window and held out her arm. The bird squawked and flew across and landed first on the windowsill and then hopped onto her arm.

'*Olá!*' crooned the bird.

'So you're back!' laughed Alice, thrilled to see him again.

Alice's Blog #4:

Monday 19th February 2018

At last someone has responded to my blog. Well, it's more than just someone, it's the actual designer of the C-Bean, a lady called Karla Ingermann from Germany! You can read what she wrote in the column next to this one, but the most important thing she told me was that we can't leave the C-Bean out of action for more than a hundred days, or its operating system will lock up and stop working altogether. Anyway, Karla says she is prepared to come over and help us get it going again. As it's already been a week since the C-Bean got stuck, that leaves us ninety-three days to fix it. At least that's two more weeks than we've got to come up with the money for the island.

So Charlie and I are trying to think of how to persuade Mr McLintock to pay for it to be rescued off the rocks where we got stranded, and get it brought back to our schoolyard. Even then it might not work any more, but I think it's worth a try. I know Dr Foster wants us to get the C-Bean back, but he says it will cost a lot, and right now the islanders are only concerned about buying the island, so there isn't going to be any spare money for the C-Bean.

My head is finally feeling better – they say I bruised my skull really quite badly, and that I've got to go for a special test in Glasgow, to make sure everything is all right. They are going to put me in a scanner thing and take pictures of my brain in slices. But it's only to make sure – Mum says she thinks I'm perfectly fine.

Dad says the launch phase of the wave energy plant is going well – the machines are now properly anchored out in the sea to the west of St Kilda, where the biggest, strongest waves are, and it's already generating power. But it's not yet hooked up to the part that actually collects the power and feeds it into the National Grid – that's the part Dad is working on now. We hardly see him at the moment because he's always working down in the shed.

There is one worrying thing that's happened: the cylinder containing the mercury, which we brought back with us from Hong Kong, has been washed up on the beach. Charlie found it, but unfortunately the lid had come off and the thing was completely empty. So somehow all the mercury got into the sea during the storm. This is not good news, especially after finding the dead birds on the other side of the island. It might take years, they say, for the grass and the sea to recover, and for the fish and birds to re-establish themselves.

Also, about the gold nugget: we couldn't tell Dr Foster, but it is real. If we could just think up a way to sell it, the money we'd get for it would pay for everything: the rest of the money needed to buy the island, and depending what we get, maybe enough to pay to rescue the C-Bean and get it fixed.

I've had one idea, but it might not work. I am thinking about telling my sister Lori, because she is going to meet us in Glasgow when I go for my scan, and while Mum and I are at the hospital, perhaps she could go and sell it to a gold dealer or something.

Tuesday 20th February 2018

There was a huge commotion in Village Bay today: Spex came running up to the houses barking his head off before it was even light, and nobody knew what was the matter with him. He kept running down towards the water and then running back again. Mr McLintock went down to the beach in the dark with his torch to take a look. He came running back and woke up the whole village. Spex was right: there was an emergency. A female minke whale was beached on the shore. Dad and I got down to the beach a few minutes after Charlie and his dad. The whale seemed very confused and didn't have the strength to push herself back into the water.

'It must have happened at about 2 am when it was high tide,' Charlie's dad said. 'I think it's important to keep the whale's skin wet until the next high tide this afternoon, and then there's a chance she could get back into the water and swim away.'

Mr McLintock went to get his truck and his fire hose. The men connected the hose to a pump from the Evaw sheds. It just about stretched as far as the little inlet of seawater at the side of the bay, but only if they sprayed the water high into the air, and then it more or less landed on the whale.

Edie's mum's managed to take samples of blood from the whale to send to the environmentalists at the lab on the mainland. While she pushed a hypodermic needle into its thick browny-grey skin, I stroked the side of the whale. It mostly felt soft and rubbery but there were rough patches where barnacles had attached themselves to her skin.

The minke whale was at least ten metres long and lying on her side, so every time she blew air out of her blow-hole, the people standing on that side of her got a blast of warm fishy air. But the smell wasn't nearly as disgusting as being shut in the C-Bean with a durian.

All morning the men kept on spraying her with water. I asked Charlie's dad why he thought the whale had got stranded, and he said sometimes it's just that they're ill, sometimes they get confused by deep-sea signals from submarines, but nowadays they think it's more likely to be because of poisonous chemicals in the sea water. That was what I was afraid he would say. I remembered the man in Melbourne giving the speech saying whales can get disorientated due to mercury poisoning. I felt terrible: what if the mercury from our cylinder had got into this whale's body or brain while it was feeding in the bays around St Kilda?

By about one o'clock in the afternoon the tide was coming in fast, and the whale started to try and move herself with her fins. We were all soaking wet and frozen, but no one was prepared to leave the beach until we had done everything we could to get her back in the water. Then, by my watch, at 1.28pm she was finally afloat again, and swam off into the deeper water of the bay, blowing out through her hole very happily.

Dad said, 'Right, I don't know about you lot, but I'm off to have a nice hot bath!' Everyone laughed, and we all went back up to the village.

So we have successfully performed one rescue operation, but rescuing the C-Bean is now really urgent. We only have a couple of months to think of something.

Today I had a meeting with Charlie, Edie, and the others during school lunch break and we decided that we should definitely try to sell the gold nugget. Sam F took lots of pictures of it this afternoon with his camera so he would remember it, and then I brought it home in my schoolbag. Tomorrow Mum and I are being taken by helicopter for my head scan in Glasgow. So tonight I am going to phone Lori while Mum and Dad are out at an islanders' meeting in the pub.

Tonight is also the first time I am babysitting for Kit – Mum says he'll be an angel, that it's only for a couple of hours and he's usually asleep by seven, so I should manage OK.

Wednesday 21st February

Kit was not much of an angel. He cried pretty much the whole time his mum and dad were gone, and I still had to phone Lori. I had Kit on my lap feeding him with a bottle in one hand, and the phone in the other. Lori didn't answer the first time, so I left a message, and then she rang me back. She said she was in the tuck shop getting some sweets when I rang.

'Lucky you,' I said, 'I've got stuck with your baby brother and he won't stop crying.' Just to prove it, Kit let out a particularly loud yell at that point, and then Lori went quiet.

I don't usually ask my sister for help, it's only something I'd do when I'm desperate. For one thing, she'd want to know all about the C-Bean, and how on earth we got this gold nugget, and I didn't want to have to tell her everything. But I knew I needed her help.

I took a deep breath. 'Lori, you know how the islanders need another hundred thousand pounds to buy the island?'

'Yes.'

'And it would be cool, wouldn't it, if we could help make it happen?'

'Yes. Where is this leading, Alice?'

'Well, I've got a sort of winning lottery ticket, and I need you to help me cash it in while we are in Glasgow tomorrow.'

In the end it was that simple – she just said yes! What I didn't tell her, though, was the lottery ticket weighs 2.5 kilogrammes and is made of solid gold. I'll have to find a way to tell Lori that tomorrow.

Thursday 22nd February 2018

Mum kept the helicopter waiting twenty minutes while she explained everything to Edie's mum about Kit's routine and made sure she'd left enough milk for him. I could tell she was cross with Dad because at first he said he would take me to Glasgow, but when he lost all of Tuesday because of the minke whale, he said he had slipped behind on his schedule and needed to make up the time if they were going to start the wave energy plant by the end of April.

The pilot was not very pleased about being kept waiting either, but he still said I could sit in the front next to him, which was really exciting. Dr Foster brought my classmates out to watch us go. I made a thumbs-up sign to them and pointed to my bag so they knew I'd got the gold nugget with me. The island slipped away from under us as the helicopter swooped into the sky, tail first. I could see the whole village spread out below across the mountainside, just like the map, with scatterings of sheep and stone cleitean. After a while you couldn't tell which was which. Then I could see over the ridge and down into Gleann Mor, where the sea didn't look too oily in the early morning sunshine. The last thing I saw was the smooth black sides of the C-Bean wedged between the white and grey rocks. As we flew higher, I could see that it was already covered in bird poo.

Lori was looking pretty anxious in her pink jacket with the collar turned up and her hair blowing in the wind when we landed on the huge 'H' on the roof of Glasgow General Hospital. I managed to get her on her own when we went to the toilets, while Mum talked to one of the nurses about the tests I was having.

Straight away, while we were still walking along the corridor, Lori was asking, 'Where's the lottery ticket then? What kind is it? How do you know how much you've won? The newsagents don't have much cash in their tills, you know. You don't really know how it works, Alice.'

I took a deep breath and said, 'This is not a normal lottery ticket.'

'What is it then?' Lori was getting impatient.

I pulled her inside the first toilet cubicle, opened my bag so she could see the gold nugget. At first she just stared at it, and then she laughed.

'What the hell is that, Alice?'

'It's 2.5 kilogrammes of pure solid gold that we found in one of the stone cleitean on the island and it's worth about forty thousand pounds a kilo so Edie calculated that it should sell for over a hundred thousand pounds,' I lied without even pausing for breath.

'Whoah there! Don't be an idiot, Alice. Let me get this right: you want me to just walk into somewhere, hand over this lump of metal, and say, here, weigh this, and convert it into cash please?'

'More or less, yes. But a cheque would be safer, made out to The New St Kilda Trust Fund.'

Lori was silent, then finally she said, 'OK, I'll give it a go.'

Five hours later I was in the helicopter flying back to St Kilda with a huge cheque in my purse and an even bigger smile on my face. Mum thought it was because I'd been told my brain was fine. She said I'd been very brave. Little did she know that my brain was actually on fire after what had happened.

Lori is so cool I still can't believe it! She found out there was some antique metal dealer in a little back street in Glasgow and took it there. She told them she had been left the nugget by her great-great-uncle, who used to be a gold prospector in Australia. Once they had checked it was real gold, they wrote her the cheque there and then.

When she handed it to me, she said, 'Alice, you're starting to seem really grown up all of a sudden. You're not so much of a kid sister any more.' I beamed, and told her I was really proud of her too, and we hugged each other.

Charlie, Dad and Edie were waiting to meet us off the helicopter. It was dark when we landed, and Hannah and both Sams were already in bed. I wanted them to all be there when I told them, but for now I couldn't even tell Edie and Charlie with both my parents there. I just kept the huge smile on my face, and tapped the side of my nose knowingly. I made a money sign by rubbing my fingers together. Charlie raised his eyebrows: how much? I signed two ones and four zeros at him. He shook his wrist in approval, like he'd touched something very hot, and Edie clapped her hands. I've never seen them both so excited.

It was only later, as I stared at the long number - £110,000 – on the cheque under my duvet, that it occurred to me that it must have been Old Jim who secretly donated the £500,000. That's what he had been trying to tell me on my birthday when he wrote in his notebook. But where he got the money from, I have no idea.

Friday 23rd February 2018

This morning, before Dr Foster arrived at school I showed the others the cheque for the New St Kilda Trust Fund. We were all so excited none of us could concentrate properly all day. We've decided to put it in an envelope addressed to Mr McLintock, but we're going to give it to Mrs Butterfield in the shop to give to Mr Butterfield, who will deliver it tomorrow morning. We'll tell Mrs Butterfield it came on the ferry and got mixed up with Dad's Evaw post.

As far as the minke whale was concerned, however, today was no laughing matter – the whale's blood showed up not just mercury, but lots of other toxic chemicals from the sea too. She could easily get beached again on another island, where there might be nobody to help her that time.

Saturday 24th February 2018

Our plan worked, and by lunchtime everyone in the pub was apparently talking about the second cheque that had arrived from an anonymous donor. Mr McLintock was so happy, he proposed a toast 'To All the New St Kilda Islanders!'

Then Dad proposed another toast 'To the Future of St Kilda', and beer slopped everywhere as they all clunked glasses. No one could really believe that the island was now ours.

When Dr Foster saw our faces looking through the window, he called us all inside and proposed a third toast, 'To the Children of St Kilda'. The pub erupted with a loud 'Hear, hear!' Everyone on the island has been really nice to us since we were rescued from the rocks. They all said the storm must have been much worse than they thought to have blown our wee classroom onto the rocks like that.

Then Dr Foster stood up and made a speech. He said that he wanted to thank the people of St Kilda for making him feel so welcome here. There were more shouts of 'Hear hear!' again as well as 'Get on with it, Adrian!' Dr Foster took another sip of his beer, and then said, 'So, in the interests of all our kids, I think the extra ten thousand quid we've been sent should be spent getting their classroom winched off the cliff, fixed up and returned to the school yard.'

Mr McLintock slapped him on the back, and said loudly, 'A grand idea. So be it!'

By the end of the afternoon, the celebrations in the pub had turned into a full-on party. The grown-ups drank even more whisky than they did at Hogmanay, and when it got dark someone let off a few fireworks. Even Spex and Old Jim came out to watch them. Spex barked at every single one.

I was sitting on the seawall down by the harbour rocking my baby brother in his buggy, and eating fresh chocolate éclairs from the shop with Charlie, Edie, Hannah and the two Sams, while Spix flew around making Kit laugh by squawking 'olá olá'. It was our own little celebration: soon we would have our C-Bean back again and have other adventures. For now, we were happy to watch the last of the fireworks in the night sky.

We all agreed they weren't nearly as good as the fireworks we'd seen in the other St Kilda, but right now there was nowhere we'd rather be in the whole world than right here on our own little island.

Reading Guide to SeaBEAN
Suggestions for class/reading group discussions

1. Alice lives as part of a small, isolated island community, living there because of the wave energy project. How is their lifestyle captured in the book, and what challenges do they face on a day-to-day basis?

2. The C-Bean is an imaginary piece of futuristic interactive technology: do you think the children visit the places in reality, or does it conjure up a very convincing kind of virtual reality?

3. Some of the book is written in the form of a blog written by Alice. What purpose does this serve in terms of telling the story? How does it feel different from the chapters written in the author's voice/third person?

4. Spex the dog and Spix the parrot feature strongly in the children's adventures. What part do they play in terms of plot and character development?

5. The adventures in SeaBean reveal several ways in which humans exploit and damage nature and the Earth's eco-systems: what do you think is the most important discovery Alice and her schoolmates make?

6. The children do not always tell the adults in the story the whole truth: when do you think they were wrong to do so, and why do you think they felt they could not tell their parents at the time what was going on?

7. St Kilda is a real place where at the moment no one lives all year round. How does the story integrate and make use of the different aspects of the actual island such as its geography, its wildlife and its history?

8. How is time handled in the book? Do things happen in a chronological sequence; how do they know about time differences between places?

9. In what way does Alice's relationship with her friends and family change over the course of the book? What does she learn about herself?

10. Think about the use of colour, atmosphere and sound in relation to the moment of arrival in each new place the C-Bean transports them to: how is the setting for each adventure established?

11. The protagonist (main character) in the adventure story genre often starts out from the ordinary/known world and enters an extraordinary/unknown one, where they are challenged to resolve certain issues and bring home the 'treasure' or 'elixir'. How is this organised and paced in SeaBean? What do you think represents the treasure from Alice's point of view?

12. The novel starts with a Prologue. What role does this play in your understanding of the main story?

What readers say about SeaBEAN

Think Secret Island meets Dr Who's Tardis and Greenpeace Junior. This non-stop adventure will excite imaginations and stimulate eco-debates to leave young readers asking when SeaBEAN 2 is coming.

Rt Hon Ed Davey MP
Secretary of State for Engergy and Climate Change

It's a different way of introducing children to environmental issues and I wish you every success with it. I think the thermochromic cover is a great idea.

Dame Jacqueline Wilson DBE FRSL

I really enjoyed reading this novel, inspired by a place I know and love very much. It's always really interesting to see how other people view St Kilda; it's landscape and history and how this inspires them. Sarah Holding has very cleverly woven contemporary issues and concerns affecting St Kilda, Scotland and the world into a great kids' adventure story. Although St Kilda is remote it is, and always has been, affected by the wider world. Today we monitor the seabird colonies and see many species declining in part due to changes in the temperature of the ocean as well as an increase in marine pollutants. It is difficult to imagine St Kilda without it's seabirds, in fact it would not be St Kilda without the vast colonies of gannet, fulmar and puffin that sustained the community for thousands of years. I hope this book inspires people to care for the world we live and to see the interconnectedness of our lives with the global environment and, of course, to take special care of St Kilda.

Susan Bain
Western Isles Manager, National Trust for Scotland

I love the way that the SeaBEAN can do anything and allows them to travel around the world. I particularly like the talking parrot and the dog – Spix and Spex. The cover is cool when it heats up to show the sea, clouds and lightening. I can't wait for the next two books!

Ellen Barnette
aged 10

SeaWAR

SARAH HOLDING

SeaWAR
Part 2 of the SeaBEAN Trilogy

It's the year 1918: Left broken and beyond repair after
their fateful last trip, the C-Bean is being fixed and gets
accidentally sent back in time. When Alice performs
a reset., things don't go exactly as planned. Before
they know it, Alice and her new wartime companions
embark on a journey through time to solve some dark
secrets from St Kilda's past and safeguard the future.

Chapter 1: Reset

It was 8 a.m. on 15 May 2018, half an hour before school was due to start, and Alice wandered down the village street early with her bright blue parrot Spix following her all the way. A fine Scottish rain had been falling since first light. Alice was daydreaming about the C-Bean again, and how she'd got it to open that first day it arrived on the beach. She remembered how it recorded everything about her, then projected her holographic image which talked back in her voice, and how she only had to imagine something and it would magically appear a few seconds later in a small recess in the wall.

Alice found herself alone in the schoolyard. She walked round and round the C-Bean's four walls, singing an old Gaelic sea shanty they'd just learned and trailing her hand over its crusty ruined surface, which looked worse than ever. More worrying was the fact that the tiny door concealing the access panel had come open and, when Alice looked more closely, she saw the cardkey was missing from the slot and a peculiar message was flashing across the tiny LED screen:

1-NVAL-1-DC-0-MMANDKR-0-B2-0-9-0-RE-5-ET-0-RAB-0-RT

Still humming the sea shanty, Alice closed her eyes and touched the keypad. She flinched. The buttons were burning hot but, as she ran her fingers lightly over them, one by one they seemed to buzz slightly in response.

'Come on C-Bean, you can do it. Remember me, Alice. Your friend?'

She opened her eyes a crack and thought she was imagining it at first. Was one of the lights on the panel glowing faintly? The keys were cooler to her touch now, and seemed softer somehow, like skin. She hummed the song again softly, like a lullaby, and very slowly the row of lights starting pulsing red and green in sequence. Alice smiled a secret smile, and kept singing to the C-Bean, coaxing it back to life. After a few minutes it was humming the same pattern of notes back to her, very quietly, but definitely making its own sounds. Alice could already see the sores nearest to the access panel were starting to heal – at least, she was sure the oozing substance was turning a darker blue-black.

She wanted to run into the office and tell Karla, but she didn't dare leave the C-Bean at this critical moment of its recovery. Nor did she want to shout for Karla to come, in case the noise upset the C-Bean, so she stayed by its side until she could see Charlie taking a shortcut to school across the machair. She beckoned wildly to him. When he got near, she whispered breathlessly, 'Charlie, go and get Karla, tell her something's happening.'

Karla was on a conference call to Germany for what seemed like a long time. The children were listening to her talking from the schoolroom, unable to concentrate on their work, but none of them could understand any of the conversation. All they knew was that Karla seemed very excited and kept sneezing and repeating the words 'biomimetische funktion'. After she got off the phone, she came into the classroom and told them that she had realised that some rather experimental things got added to the design of the C-Bean during its production process.

'Why was that Karla?' asked Charlie.

'I beleef it was in order to get around a few ... malfunctions it had defeloped.'

The Sams started giggling because of her accent, Hannah meanwhile was drawing a picture of Karla, and Edie was sitting with her arms folded looking suspicious, as usual.

'What kind of experimental things?' asked Alice.

'Exactly as you found out – it responds to human varmth and touch and soothing sounds. Who thought it vood be possible? Karla seemed completely amazed, and it made her accent stronger and more difficult to understand, perhaps because she was thinking too much in German.

'I knew about that the first time I found the C-Bean,' murmured Alice, almost to herself.

Alice was sent to get some more tissues for Karla from the shop, but when she came back, she couldn't resist loitering by the C-Bean for a while longer in the schoolyard.

'You can do it,' she breathed, her face very close to one of its walls. She touched one of the ridges of weird rust along a seam. To her amazement, the rust started to shrink very gradually under her fingertips. She slowly worked her way round all four sides until it had all but vanished. Just as the last particles of rust disappeared, the door of the C-Bean clicked open. Alice smiled, took a deep breath and stepped inside.

There was a mouldy fishy smell inside, like a pair of wellington boots that have been left with seawater inside. The walls were going green and mouldy, but when Alice ran her hands over them it didn't seem to make the mould disappear at all. So instead Alice stood in the middle of the pod with her eyes closed and focused her thoughts on the most pristine clean white bed sheets she'd ever seen, until she could picture them blowing and billowing in the wild St Kilda wind, smelling sharply of the fresh crisp air. After a while she didn't need to imagine the clean smell, she just knew the C-Bean was producing it itself, completely blotting out the fishy smell, and it had added in the sounds of the waves and seagulls to complete the atmosphere. When Alice opened her eyes again, the walls were bright and alive. She was surrounded by a kaleidoscope of images from all over the island. It was as if the C-Bean was happy to be home and was busily sorting through its memory bank. Alice clapped her hands with joy, and ran out to get Karla.

By the time all the children trooped inside the C-Bean, Spix tagging along with them, it was replaying its own rescue, a silent witness to its own sea adventure, like a film shot from the pod's point of view as it came in to land. The children could see old Jim up on the hillside in his ragged black clothes watching, as well as a colourful bunch of children shouting and waving on the beach, right up until the cable started to break and it almost dropped into the sea.

'Look, it's us!' chorused the Sams in unison.

Then the walls went blank again. Spix squawked loudly as if in protest.

'Hmm, not quite fixed then,' Edie couldn't resist saying.

'Oh come on Edie, it was quite traumatic for the C-Bean, nearly getting dropped like that,' ventured Alice. Disappointed, the other children drifted back to class, but Alice stayed, her curiosity working overtime.

Karla went back to the office and brought her laptop. She sat down cross-legged on the floor, scrolling through its lines of computer code, looking for something in particular. Spix was fidgeting around on the floor, taking sunflower seeds from Alice's hand. Charlie came to fetch Alice.

'Hey, your mum says you can't spend all day in here.'

Just then, the C-Bean started making a low crackling sound and the same complicated code – masses and masses of black symbols and numbers like secret instructions – began moving up the walls around them. Suddenly one line that was highlighted in bright yellow appeared near the floor. The C-Bean locked onto that one piece of information and then began duplicating the single line of code so it appeared on every surface, getting larger and larger. They all stared in amazement.

'Look!' said Charlie, 'It's worked it out for you Karla. That's where the problem is.'

Karla looked up and smiled for the first time ever. When she glanced back at her laptop the same line of code on her screen had been highlighted, and it appeared the C-Bean was busy making alterations by itself. The code was changing before her very eyes, without her needing even to touch the keyboard.

'Charlie, can you be a kind one and go back to my office to get my mobile phone? I again must call ze guys in Germany right zis moment!'

Charlie ran off to get it and Alice started singing her song again, happy in the knowledge that the C-Bean might actually work. She could feel the wind picking up outside, coming down off the highest mountain, Conachair, into Village Bay to meet the incoming waves. It whistled round the schoolyard, as if it too was as impatient and excited as Alice felt. A sudden gust whipped up against the broken door of the C-Bean and banged it shut. Spix let out a loud squawk. A shudder ran through the pod's structure, and the walls went dark.

Karla sniffed loudly and then cleared her throat in the dimness. Alice could still see her face in the glow from the laptop screen.

'Alice, please to check ze door for me.' There was a tiny note of panic in her voice.

Alice crawled on her hands and knees towards the door. She realized at that moment she too felt quite anxious. There was a thin line of daylight visible along one side where the door didn't fit properly anymore. The last time she'd had to crawl like this in the pod was when it had got stuck on the rocks coming back from Australia and she'd banged her head badly. She was just about to reach out for the door when the C-Bean started shivering. Soon the whole room was vibrating and quivering. Karla's laptop slid off her lap and across the floor then crashed into the wall opposite and stopped working. Alice stood up carefully in the dark and tried to push open the door, but it was stuck fast. They were trapped inside – unless Charlie could get it open again from the outside.

It was not easy trying to think with the C-Bean shaking so much. Alice sat on the floor and tried to calm it down, making the *shhh shhh* sounds she used to soothe her baby brother Kit. It was making her feel quite nauseous. She could hear Karla trying to get the laptop to boot again. Alice closed her eyes. There was another noise building up from somewhere, like a radio or TV that wasn't tuned in properly, something Alice knew was called white noise. It crackled and buzzed louder and louder. Karla started pummeling the door with her fists and calling.

'Charlie, Charlie, ve are stuck! Help! Alice, ve are going to need to do a factory reset, now, quickly!'

'How do we do that?' asked Alice, trying to remain calm.

'Reset the date and time. Sorry, but I get very – how do you say it – claustrophobic. I don't like to be in small confined spaces. It makes me panic.'

Alice concentrated very hard on the word 'reset' in her mind. She laid out each letter individually as if she was making the word in plastic tiles. As she put the 't' at the end, a glowing white rectangle appeared out of the gloom like a letterbox on the back of the C-Bean's door. In the white rectangle was a single vertical line, a cursor that blinked on and off. Karla stared in amazement.

'It vants us to input something,' she said impatiently, 'but vat?'

Alice thought for a moment and then uttered a string of numbers, barely audible over the white noise.

'Fifteen, zero five, eighteen.'

The numbers appeared dutifully one by one behind the blinking cursor, and then paused. The C-Bean had steadied itself, and was now just rocking slightly to and fro. They both stared at the digits and waited. Nothing happened.

'It isn't vorking!' wailed Karla.

'Oh,' said Alice, realizing her mistake, 'Reset.'

There was a sharp jolt and the C-Bean's door flew open. The pod's interior was suddenly flooded with sunlight, and they both squinted. Karla stood up and exhaled slowly, like she'd been holding her breath the whole time it had been wedged shut, and then ran out of the door. Spix rearranged his tail feathers and followed after her. Alice stood in the doorway, her eyes still adjusting to the brightness.

What with the wind and all the shuddering and quivering, the C-Bean had moved quite a long way from the schoolyard and it was now down by the shoreline facing the water, in almost the same place where it was nearly dropped in the sea by the helicopter. The waves were breaking a few metres from the base of the pod. Alice groaned as she realised another winching was going to be necessary. However, miraculously, the problem with the door seemed to have been rectified – she found she could now click it shut behind her, no problem. She was just wondering how they would afford to move it all over again, when Karla came running back.

'Vere are ve?' she cried, looking confused and somewhat stricken. Alice thought the claustrophobia must have still been affecting her.

'On St Kilda,' Alice said gently.

'*Nicht wo. Aber* - I mean VEN are ve?'

Alice looked around her. There was something odd, for sure. She counted the houses in the village and found that there were six missing. Above the village, there was no concrete road winding up to the radar station on the ridge, just a dirt track. There was also no gun emplacement on the headland. And when she turned and looked out to sea, she couldn't see the wave energy station either. Some things were where they should be though – the little walled graveyard, the school, the chapel, and further up the slope, she could make out the entrance to Old Jim's underground house.

'Erm. Let's go up to the schoolhouse and find the others,' Alice suggested.

They started to trudge along the beach towards the school and the chapel. As they got nearer, a bell started ringing. A handful of children ran out of the classroom into the yard. Alice waved. But her classmates looked very unfamiliar somehow. They had all dressed up in olden-days clothes, the girls were wearing white smocks over brown dresses, and the boys were wearing shorts and caps and hand-knitted woollen sweaters. Then it occurred to Alice that it wasn't their clothing that made them seem unfamiliar – these were not the St Kildan children she knew. She studied their faces. No Edie, Hannah, Charlie or a Sam among them. She stopped walking and stood still.

'Vat is wrong?' Karla asked.

'I'm not sure,' said Alice, 'But I think resetting the C-Bean has altered the clock a bit too much.'

SeaWAR

ISBN: 978-1-909339-07-1
ePub ISBN: 978-1-909339-10-1

Visit The SeaBEAN Trilogy site

LOOK OUT FOR
Part 3 of the
SeaBEAN Trilogy

SeaRISE

SARAH HOLDING

SeaRISE
Part 3 of the SeaBEAN Trilogy

ISBN: 978-1-909339-08-8
ePub ISBN: 978-1-909339-11-8

It's the year 2118: Alice and her schoolmates find they have been summoned to the future in the C-Bean and imprisoned there by its inventor. Realising they must now know too much, yet trapped in a world they no longer understand, they have to plan an escape route back to the present before it's too late and the planet is ruined forever.

 Visit The SeaBEAN Trilogy site

 Visit the author's Facebook page

 Visit Medina Publishing Ltd

How does the cover of the SeaBEAN book reveal an image when touched?

The covers of the SeaBEAN Trilogy are printed like a normal book, but another very special ink is then printed on top. This special ink is called a leuco dye and is thermochromic, which means it changes its appearance when the temperature changes.

SeaBEAN has been printed with a black leuco dye that goes from black to clear at just under 37 degrees Celsius (which is normal body temperature). The dye is composed of pigment particles with a solvent that melts at a certain temperature. When the cover is warm from the body heat from your hand – or your teacup, or the sun – the solvent is in its melted form and the pigment particles don't join with each other, allowing you to see through to the picture behind. When the book cover is cold the solvent is solid and the lueco dye particles join together to form a black coating so you can't see what is underneath.

Visit http://www.colorchange.com/leuco-dyes